# FLOWERS, FELONS, & FAMILIES

Lucia Kuhl

# Contents

# CHAPTER 1

Hallelujah! One more consultation and I was free. The double-sided gate to Raymont Manor stood open. It had been almost four decades since I'd last driven down the winding tree-tunneled lane to the big house, which looked more like a castle with its red brick, turrets, and ivy than a house. The manor sat nestled on its own private lake in St. Joseph County, just across the one-and-a-half-lane road from LaPorte County in Northern Indiana.

"Whew, Sampson, we are good so far. No dead bodies," I said to the chocolate Labrador Retriever puppy beside me as the black wrought-iron gate appeared in my rear-view mirror. His nose was plastered to the slightly opened window, sniffing every available scent. No bodies, what a relief. A huge relief.

The sun glistened off paper-thin ice patches on Raymont Lake to my right. The old rope swing twisted in the slight breeze. Oh, how I had loved that swing. It beckoned my inner child to play, but my dashboard thermometer read 50 degrees in early March. Much too cold to swing out over the water.

A white bunny hopped into the middle of my path, shaking his little head. Sampson responded with a low growl and slapped my arm with his tail.

"Thanks, Sampson. I so needed that."

I was late. I was always late. Not because I didn't plan, but I was always lost. GPS and I had issues. It never knew where it was, and it hated me. I'd tried using my phone and all the portable devices on the market. No dice. GPS and I were not meant to be together.

This time, I thought I knew where I was going. This time, I thought I'd arrive on time. I was so wrong.

I checked the clock on my dashboard. I was only thirty minutes late. And I had texted Bonnie Crescent Home-scaping's scheduler to ask her to notify Mr. Raymont.

Would Mr. Raymont remember me after all these years? How would I explain to him I was late because I'd gotten lost? As children, he'd lectured his daughter and me about the importance of punctuality. I recalled the lesson. Through the years, it looped in my mind. What could I say? Universal forces conspired against me.

Rounding the last twist, the Manor came into view. I'd been here dozens of times, but I was twelve, and four decades later, the state moved the roads. Roads are supposed to be permanent things. Something you can count on. Stable, always there for you. Yes, there is always road construction, but typically, they don't move whole road groupings. This time, they had.

I parked the car in front of the manor's grand entrance. Funny, in my decades as a Feng Shui Practitioner, I'd worked in some extravagant houses. Double, triple, even quadrupled the price. I expected Raymont Manor to look small, but it still held the same wide-eyed wonder from my youth. Pieces of glorious memories darted across my mental screen, and a smile and happy tears found a place on my face. Raymont Manor held my best childhood memories.

Back then, the twenty-minute trip from our house in Abracadabra, Indiana, to The Manor felt like hours, but when my parent's or grandparent's car pulled to the door, Lizzie, her mom, and Mr. Raymont were always outside to greet me before the car stopped.

Today, the front door remained closed. Mr. Raymont didn't know that Faith from Crescent Homescaping was Little Faith Bracken, who used to sit in the middle of his workbench, chattering away.

The woman exiting her rented Mercedes in his driveway was now fifty-plus and the top consultant at the exorbitantly priced New York, Santa Barbara, and L.A. Homescaping firm. I scanned the front landscaping and climbed the wheaten-colored stone steps to the massive front castle door. Hmm. They'd installed a Ring Doorbell. Technology had invaded history. I liked the old one better. It had an ominous sound. Reminded me of a doorbell Lurch should answer.

No answer.

Hmmm.

Not good.

The Mr. Raymont I remembered was not the type to blow you off. If he were angry because you were late, he'd let you know in about three words. If he was glad to see you, everybody—friend or soon-to-be friend—received a big bear hug.

Maybe he was out back. He'd always had a workshop in the backyard. It smelled of sawdust and his unique mixture of varnish.

Should I walk around back? I was surprising him.

Because my schedule consisted of stops in Florida, Nashville, Indianapolis, and Chicago, our scheduler had placed Mr. Raymont on my calendar at the last minute. I didn't tell Bonnie Mr. Raymont was an old friend. The less Gabby-Mouth knew, the better.

In exchange, Bonnie moved the Chicago client to my nemesis in the company. Fine with me. I needed to escape on vacation. I was never coming back. But Blabbermouth didn't need to know that. No one needed to know that yet. I was done.

Anyhow, I rarely got to work for people from my childhood. Mr. Raymont was my second since I'd joined the company decades ago. I followed the sidewalk around the house. They'd added two Orangeola Weeping Japanese Maples to the yard since I'd been here last. Nice touch. I highly approved. Yard and Garden Feng Shui are my specialties, but I'm fluent in all aspects of Feng Shui. Over the years I'd been in the business, I'd developed my own special style.

I scanned the pool area and back terrace. No Mr. Raymont. Where was the ubiquitous housekeeper and gardener? I'd never been to The Manor when there weren't at least a few house staff here.

"Mr. Raymont," I yelled.

No answer.

I knocked on the door of his workshop. A machine ran inside. I knocked again. No answer. He probably couldn't hear over the machine's noise. I opened the door. Mr. Raymont's body thudded at my feet. So much for no dead bodies.

# CHAPTER 2

I should have screamed or cried or both. Unlike the others, I knew Mr. Raymont personally. He was my 'other father.' The one who was there when Vito wasn't. Why didn't grief pour out of me?

Because I'd seen enough dead bodies lately, I didn't have anything left inside me. I couldn't deal with more police. I'd had enough of them too. To be honest, I had just about enough of everything except Sampson. I fell deeper in love with his cute little puppy face every day.

Don't get me wrong, I'm not against the police, but I knew law enforcement thought I was a serial killer. Like I would kill and then call the police. Really? And worse yet, I would kill my clients one after another. They obviously thought I was either incredibly brazen or stupid. Stupid topped their list. All I wanted was to finish the consultation and disappear. My sanity required it.

I looked at the body at my feet. I tried to feel something. All I felt was numb. What should I do now? Walk away? Let someone else find poor Mr. Raymont's body. My gut clenched at that suggestion. Someone he knew should stay with him until the police arrived. Someone.

And that someone had to be me. I needed to advocate for him. If circumstances were reversed, Mr. Raymont would have moved oceans for me. But I couldn't call the police again. It wasn't in me. The locals would call Special Agent Harvey Wallbanger.

Yes, that is his real name. I imagine the other kids bullied Harvey as a child without mercy. That's probably why he's so FOCUSED and determined. And why he's convinced I'm guilty. Maybe if I called the police, let them arrive, and then faked being sick, I could get the interview over in a flash before they connected me to the other murders. If I barfed on one of their shoes, that trick might work. Could I hurl at will? Ring Video already had my picture. I knew there was a reason I liked the old doorbell better. If I left the scene without calling, I'd look guilty.

I couldn't. I couldn't deal with another interrogation. My stomach churned while I chewed on my fingernails. There was another option, but I couldn't deal with him either. Sisters are supposed to be able to call their brothers for help, especially when their brother is a cop. A Major Crimes Detective. Anyhow, that's what I'd heard. I hadn't talked to my brother in, well, a decade, but we do share the same blood and parents. He'd objected to my "snake oil" career. I objected to his condescending comments. We hadn't spoken since that day.

I needed to make a decision. Mr. Raymont was still at my feet. What to do? Flip a coin? Open the bible to a random passage? Grab a handful of gravel and use them as Ruine stones? Spit into the wind? Oh, here's a thought. Maybe I should just call Harvey and get it over. He could put me out of my misery and haul me off to jail for crimes I didn't commit. Wouldn't that make my cop brother happy?

But who would care for Sampson? I only rescued the pup a few days ago, but already we had bonded. Sampson needed me. Seriously, what do I do?

I do the worst of two horrible options. Reaching into my pocket, I tapped Arie's cell number. It went straight to voicemail. Of course. Why would my brother answer when I needed him? Did he know how much it emotionally cost me to reach out? Sorry, Bro, you can't hide from me. If I can't get him on his cell, I'll call his business, and I'll call Major Crimes if I can't get him there.

"Nothing Fancy Garden Center, Lynn speaking," the voice on the other end of the phone said.

"Hi Lynn, this is Faith Bracken. I don't know if you remember me. I'm Arie's sister. I need to speak to him right away." Lynn took a few seconds to respond. What had my dear brother told her about me? Truth be told, I was the most normal, least damaged family member. Of course, he would not see it that way. I sold "snake oil."

"Sorry, Faith. He's not here. I assume you've already tried his cell. So, try the station." She gave me the number.

"Thanks, Lynn. I appreciate it. If he comes in soon, will you have him call me?"

"Sure will. Everything okay? Is there something I can help you with?"

Lynn was nice. Why she worked for Arie? I shrugged. Everyone had their reasons.

"No, but I'll handle it. Thank you."

I ended the call and dialed the phone number for the Michiana Major Crimes Task Force.

A gruff voice answered the phone.

"Major Crimes." Just his voice had me shaking in my Jimmy Choo boots. My breakfast turned and twisted as I spoke. I didn't want to do this. I needed to do this. Why was someone dropping bodies for me to find?

"This is Faith Bracken, Arie's sister." I heard my mouth say. "I need to talk to him. It's an emergency." Not really. I mean, Mr. Raymont was dead. Not much anyone could do for him.

"Hold on," the gruff voice said. He was gone for a minute or two. Arie was probably deciding whether to take my call or not and how his actions would look to the other cops.

"Hi, this is Captain Blake Bloom. Arie's not available. How can I help?"

At least he sounded friendly. He knew the word help, which is more than I expected from my brother.

"Is his partner Pete there?" From my high school Facebook friends' posts, I knew that Pete was engaged to a famous psychic. So the odds were good; Pete wouldn't hold my "snake oil" profession against me.

"No, I'm afraid Pete is with Arie. You're stuck with me."

The captain had a pleasant, soothing voice.

"Okay, well, I'm in the area on business, and I just found a dead body."

# CHAPTER 3

What should I do while I wait? I'd been hired to consult. My company had already been paid. I should do my job. But what if I destroyed some evidence while walking around or dropped something that made me look guilty? That would be bad. Probably best to just sit and wait here on this wooden bench proudly created by Mr. Raymont in his younger days. Or maybe I could pace in front of this bench. Pacing felt better.

I had rolled the windows down part of the way. Sampson would be fine for now. Arie's boss said someone would be here soon. Would that someone be my brother?

I longed for a brother who would put his arms around me and take away all I had been through. A brother who would make it okay. Arie hadn't been that brother in decades.

What was his boss's name again? Something flower. Bloom. Captain Bloom.

I must have walked the equivalent of five miles in the space of about eight feet before I heard the slam of one car door. Sampson barked.

"Faith," the baritone voice I recognized from the phone called. Captain Bloom was here.

So far, Arie was not. At least my brother wouldn't be the first cop I had to face. Would Bloom advocate for his subordinate's sister or lock me away forever? At this point, did it really matter? Did I care?

Yes, I did. I had goals, and some crazy lunatic serial killer was not going to rob me of those dreams. I'd made a life for myself despite my family, and no one would take it away from me. I needed to remember that when they interviewed me.

"Back here. Follow the sidewalk around the house." My stomach clenched with anxiety. My anxiety manifested as if every nerve was plugged into an outlet. The inside of my body shook while the outside remained still. I hated anxiety.

Less than a minute later, a six-foot-two rugged, sandy-haired man with blue eyes came running towards me dressed in jeans and a brown windbreaker with letters on the right front pocket. Wow! Bet the ladies enjoyed his press conferences.

His eyes traveled from me to the body and then scanned the surrounding area.

"Faith, I'm Captain Blake Bloom. Are you hurt?"

I shook my head.

"No, I opened the door, and he fell out." Wow, that sounded horrible. My nonchalant attitude probably made me look guilty. At the least, it probably made me look callous. I mean, here I was driving a Mercedes in $1,200 boots and a $5,000 jacket.

"What brought you here?" Captain Bloom asked.

"I am a Feng Shui Practitioner. Mr. Raymont had bought and paid for a consultation. Do you know what Feng Shui is?"

He laughed. "Are you asking because I'm a guy or because you think I'm a hick?"

I shrugged. "Lots of people still don't know what a Feng Shui Practitioner does."

He stood beside me. Even at 5'10, I felt like a shrimp.

"My ex-wife threw out ninety percent of my things, including me, after she read that book about keeping the things you love. I have a fair idea what you do."

Oh. Would he hold the book against me? I didn't write it.

He kneeled next to the body.

"How long ago did you find the body?"

"About five minutes before I called you. I tried Arie's cell phone and then Nothing Fancy."

He pulled a glove from his jacket pocket and felt the body.

"He's still warm. Did you check for a pulse?"

"Yes," I lied. I knew Mr. Raymont was dead. I didn't have to check, but Captain Bloom didn't need to know how I knew. Better I kept that little detail to myself.

Captain Bloom examined the woodshop door.

"What time was your appointment?"

"The appointment was for 9 AM. I arrived at 9:30. I was lost."

"I see." His voice held a hint of a chuckle. "Arie has mentioned you are directionally challenged."

I felt my nose scrunch. My brother loved to point out my faults.

"Has he now? I'm amazed he remembers."

"Where were you before you arrived here?"

And so, it started. I was a person of interest again. I'd been down this road before—too many times.

"I had breakfast at Melba's Munchies in Moon Lake from 7:45 to 8:30. I stopped at the First Source Bank in LaPorte at 9:10 to get directions, and I arrived here at 9:30." I handed him my phone. "This app tracks everything I do."

He took the phone from me.

"Okay, well, it appears you have an alibi. My guess is this man died while you were at Melba's. Good choice, by the way. Melba's cooking is the best."

"I try to eat there as often as I can when I pass this way." He looked like he was about to ask something and changed his mind.

"I've got to make some phone calls. Do you want to get your dog out of the car? We'll be here a while."

So, was that his way of detaining me without telling me he was detaining me? Was Arie on his way? Had he already run my name? Did something in some mysterious system trip and inform him I was a person of interest in multiple cases?

"Thank you for coming," I said between his phone calls. "It's nice to have someone have my back for a change." I realized as I said the words, I meant them. I'd been through a lot the last few weeks. A friendly face, even if he wasn't my friend, notched my anxiety lower.

"Arie wouldn't have it any other way."

"Oh, but he would." I handed him the keys to my car. "Just so you know, I'm not going to escape." His eyes softened, and his shoulders rounded.

I needed to get away from him, or I would cry.

# CHAPTER 4

While I waited, Sampson walked me around the front yard of Raymont Manor. He yanked me towards a lilac bush and then veered to the left to pounce in the middle of an eight-foot diameter clump of maiden grass. Some nefarious critter chattered at him from amongst the blades. Digging my feet into the mushy bluegrass, I hauled him back to me.

"Sampson, me boss. You do as I say." He sat and looked up at me with those sad, dark eyes. The "I'm sorry. It won't-happen-again look." Ten seconds later, that same white rabbit peeked from behind a rock, and Sampson lurched. Wrapping my arm around a tree, I hung on while keeping a solid hold on his leash.

"Wake up," I said, pulling my phone from the pocket of my black mercer pants. "Make a note. Puppy school." The puppy still hadn't figured out I was boss. But I'd only had him for a few days. He'd saved my butt, so I'd give him a break on his lack of manners. Poor thing had to be crated on the flight from Tennessee to Indianapolis. He sat in the Mercedes while I performed the consult in Indi and remained calm in the hotel last night before we drove the ninety miles north to our current location. I planned to swing by my property in Abracadabra and let Sampson run for a few hours before leaving for vacation. Looked like my plans needed tweaking.

Once Sampson settled down enough that I could hold my phone in my hand, walk, and talk, I decided I might as well do the job I'd been hired to do. Mr. Raymont had paid for a full consultation to determine the Chi of his grounds. I might as well give his estate the product they'd bought. The Weeping Cedar trees lining the driveway needed some serious pruning. They blocked the sun and attacked incoming vehicles, creating a depressing, almost crying energy as guests drove towards the house.

The bayberries on both sides of the steps were now considered invasive, and their prickly nature radiated prickly energy. They appeared diseased. I suggested Mock Orange bushes instead. They produce beautiful blooms and a sweet fragrance. Switching out the dying Rose of Sharon for a Korean Spice Viburnum to mix and mingle with the pines would also create a more welcoming Chi. There were a lot of wood and water elements on the grounds. The stone steps and brick helped to balance the energy.

"Wake up," I said to my phone. "Add fire element to suggestions' list." I'd write my final report when I got to wherever I was going for the night. Wonder if I'd have computer access in jail.

Working and Sampson reduced my raging anxiety from fifteen to fourteen. Maybe even thirteen. I took a minute to reconnect with the surrounding investigation.

Someone in a windbreaker had recorded my statement not long after the calvary arrived. Captain Bloom looked very adept at orchestrating the movements of all the people. As I walked, I had heard Arie's name. I surmised he'd been informed of the situation and was being updated at regular intervals.

Either Arie hated me more than I thought, or Arie must be somewhere important. My brother was an in-your-face, hands-on kind of guy. He wouldn't miss an opportunity to lecture me. My plan to slip in and out of town without seeing Arie was ruined. Thanks to my serial killer stalker. I didn't know what to call him. He arrived first. So, was I stalking him, or was he stalking me? I wasn't quite sure how that all worked.

Every so often, I'd catch Captain Bloom looking at me. Probably making sure I didn't try to make a break for it. But how could I? He'd parked right behind me. I'd given him my keys. If I were going to disappear, I'd have to do it on foot. A squad car was stationed at the front gate. Climbing over a pointed wrought iron fence was not high on my to-do list.

An hour later, my bladder said, "I need a bathroom." My watch read 1:30. My stomach said. "I'm hungry." I'd been patient. I'd been good. I really didn't want to confirm all the horrible things my brother had said about me, but enough was enough. Gathering my strength for a confrontation, I headed back towards the workshop.

"Captain Bloom, I am sorry to bother you, but I need to use the bathroom and get something to eat."

He waved off two people in windbreakers and turned to face me. He sighed.

"Can you give me just five minutes, and we'll get out of here? There's a restaurant about two miles away. You'll be staying at Arie's house tonight."

Wow, he slipped that last line in there so smoothly I almost missed it. But I didn't miss it. Like heck I was. *Don't create a scene. Be firm, but not abusive.*

"No, I won't. I'm leaving on vacation tonight."

He took a step toward me and towered over me.

"No. I'm afraid you are not. It's Arie's house or the station."

Whoa, so he wasn't so nice after all. Why was I not surprised? Indignation crept through my body. My upper teeth bit my lower lip.

"Fine," I said, "for now. Just get me out of here." Darn bladder.

# CHAPTER 5

By the time I parked in front of Arie's house, it was 3:30. Blake, as he'd told me to call him, stopped at the garden center to retrieve the key to Arie's house, giving me a few minutes to process my surroundings and fate.

Arie's place hadn't changed much except for the red metal roof.

Metal roofs were not my favorite. Red metal even less, but the house faced northwest, and two massive pine trees flanked it. The two-story house rambled a bit from various additions. Its blue siding added the water element to the energetic mix, so it wasn't the worst thing he could have done. Metal roofs tended to reflect emotional energy back at the house residents, which was good for positive emotions, not so good for depressed people. Arie had lived in a state of controlled depression for decades.

The Bowling Ball Arbs on each side of the front porch looked out of place with the rest of the landscaping. As if Arie needed to put them somewhere, and he threw two balls in the air. Where they landed, he planted.

Our grandfather had owned and operated the garden center since before Dad had been born. Gramps was an imaginative, fantastic landscaper. Both Arie and I loved plants. Grandfather had taught both of us everything our brains could absorb. Arie possessed the talent and maturity of a top-notch designer at a young age, but he'd always hated anything fussy. And that included designing for customers. He viewed anything he couldn't see, touch, hear, taste, or smell as evil. Art, creativity, design, and spirituality fell into the evil category.

When Gramps died, Arie changed the name to Nothing Fancy Garden Center and refused to do any type of landscaping. No way he'd do design. He'd sell products to people. People told him he'd be out of business in a year. That was more than a decade ago.

From the looks of things, he didn't even design for himself—just stuck stuff in the ground. His motto was 'you want a tree; I'll plant a tree. You want something fancy. GO SOMEWHERE ELSE." Gramps was probably rolling over in his grave. Since I was home, I should visit Gram and Gramps's graves. It had been a long time.

I hadn't been home for more than a drive-through visit since Gramps's funeral. I'd zipped in, dropped off treasures at my house, and proceeded to my next appointment. Now and then, I'd drop something off concerning family business at the garden center, but Arie was never around. I continued to pay the taxes on my house here in Abracadabra. Micky, a local handyman, kept it in tip-top shape and called me whenever something needed fixing.

Blake didn't need to know all that. Once he was gone, I'd move Sampson and me over to my house. It had a fenced backyard. At least, it did the last time I was through here.

Blake parked behind my Mercedes.

"Sorry, the young girl at the counter is a talker."

"Yeah, I get the feeling you're a favorite of the ladies."

His blue eyes shined at my comment.

"My charm wears off quick. People tell me I'm over-bearing."

My intuition said otherwise.

"I grew up with Arie. I think I can handle you."

I think I saw him blush. He turned and unlocked the front door, opening it for me—a stampede of negative energy charged from the house, knocking me off balance. Blake's hands closed around my waist to steady me.

I looked up into his eyes.

"Sorry, the negative vibes in here got to me."

"Just glad I was here to catch you," he said, still holding my waist.

"Yeah, me too," I mumbled under my breath.

Despite the negative energy swirling about, I managed to feel a pulse of heat between us. The man had work to do. I couldn't stay here, leaning on him forever.

"I need to open the window."

"You sure you can walk?"

"Yes, thank you." *Don't be an idiot, girl. He could lock you up in a heartbeat.*

He released me. I could stand. My legs worked. This was good. I walked through the doorway and opened the closest window after grabbing a tissue and wiping the dust off the top. Crossing the room, I opened the French doors leading to the backyard. Yeah, I know it was only fifty degrees out, but fresh air and energy were well worth a few pennies hike in the electric bill.

"When was the last time he cleaned in here?" I said, more to myself than to Blake.

"Arie's been on a tough case. Looks clean to me."

Okay, so Blake needed glasses.

"It's picked up. It's not been cleaned in ages." Did I sound like a shrew? If people understood what dust did to the energy in their homes, they'd have dust cloths surgically attached to their hands.

A streak with a fluffy plume jumped from behind the door, hopped over Sampson, turned around, and attacked my unsuspecting dog. The poor puppy yelped before pouncing on the cat. The two rolled once, and they were off chasing around the house.

"Does Arie still have his dog?"

"Yes, Liberty is the official greeter at the store."

I looked around. The place had not changed much. Just more layers of dust covered the surfaces. The need to dust and do a space clearing overwhelmed me, but I didn't want to look like a crazy person in front of the man who could put me away for the rest of my life. This was torture. Pure and simple torture. Arie was doing this on purpose.

"Good to know. Glad he has Liberty to keep him company." The conversation died for a second. "Thank You for coming to help me. I know you did it because I'm Arie's sister, but I really appreciate it. I've been on my own for a long time. It was nice to know someone had my back."

A hint of a blush spread across his face.

"Well, it's a nice back to have."

I smiled. He was already embarrassed. *Cute. But remember. He's probably going to arrest you. Do Not let your guard down.*

"Um, Arie is about ten minutes from here. Do you have luggage I can bring in for you?"

Sampson flew between us, following the white plume of a cat's tail, running and hissing at top speed.

"Sure. Let's go get my luggage."

# CHAPTER 6

As I grabbed my makeup bag out of the backseat, I watched a progressive trail of dust fly. Arie's brown SUV raced up the driveway like his pants were on fire. I walked towards the house to the sound of his car door slamming. He hadn't changed. My hand was now on the doorknob.

"Faith."

I turned to see my brother scowl. The gorilla stomped towards the house. "Are you hurt?" he asked.

I rested my back on the house for strength.

"Do you really think your boss would have brought me here if I was?"

Blake, as he asked me to call him, looked from me to Arie and back to me.

"You know what I meant."

Oh, I knew. As long as I wasn't wounded, I was fair game.

"I am not bleeding." I turned the knob and walked into the house, taking a position in front of the opened French doors. I needed the fresh energy to stabilize myself for the upcoming fight with Arie.

Arie stomped through the front door and stood between the living room and the kitchen. Blake followed him inside.

"Blake, you might as well close the door and stay a while. Arie will need someone to help him bury my body."

Blake's eyes grew wide.

"Well, I did always love a good domestic squabble."

"I'd make you some popcorn, but I doubt my brother has any food in these cupboards."

Arie's eyes narrowed.

"Faith, tell me what happened today."

"Why? You already know. Blake's been texting you off and on."

Blake's nose scrunched. "How do you...?"

"Faith is an expert at reading body language," Arie said. "Her accuracy is uncanny." Each word ripped a tear in the energy between us.

Blake crossed his arms. Arie just had to tell him. There was something good and decent about Blake. I did not want him to believe all the lies Arie was about to tell him.

"Just because I can read body language doesn't mean I use it against people."

Arie shifted his weight.

"Faith, out with it."

Fine.

"My company sent me to do a paid consultation. Since I was there to consult on the front and back yards, I reasoned my client might be in the backyard tidying things up. I arrived and rang the doorbell. No one answered. I heard a motor running in the workshop and opened the door. My client's body fell out."

"Did you arrive on time?"

"You already know the answer to that. I got lost."

"You got lost going to Raymont Manor," he said incredulously.

"Yes."

"How?"

Blake took a step forward.

"They moved the roads," I said.

"Did you ask for the assignment?"

"No. Bonnie put it on my schedule because I had a consult in Indi and one in Chicago. Raymont Manor was on my way. And for the record. Mr. Raymont did not know I was coming since my company only uses our first names. I had planned on surprising him."

Blake held a notepad in his hands.

"Wait, you didn't tell me you'd been to Raymont Manor before."

"You didn't ask. Lizzie Raymont, my friend, moved to New York to live with her mother. And I was twelve the last time I was there. It hardly seemed relevant."

From Blake's expression and body language, I knew he felt sucker punched. My stomach instantly felt queasy. Blake had a good vibe about him. How he tolerated my brother was a mystery. At that second, his phone dinged. He turned around and faced the door to read the text. He grabbed the doorknob with his other hand.

"I've got to handle this," he said without turning around. Glancing over his shoulder, Blake continued, "It was nice to meet you, Faith," and he turned the doorknob.

"Nice to meet you, Blake. Thank You for being there for me. It was comforting to have backup."

He left.

I was all alone with Arie. Not the day I had planned.

# CHAPTER 7

Arie glared at me. I glared at him.

A white tail followed by four chocolate lab paws skittered across the floor. Sampson ran smack dab into Arie's leg. My baby spun around and landed on Arie's other shoe, straining to look up Arie's 6-foot body to his face.

"Don't worry, Sampson. He likes dogs. It's me he hates. Time to go, Sampson."

Arie patted Sampson on the head.

I used the moment to pick up my makeup bag and grab the handle of my carry-on.

"Where do you think you are going?"

"I was planning to start my vacation today, but I'm taking Sampson to my house, given the events. I assume the backyard is still fenced in."

He nodded.

"It is."

"Fine, then I'll grab my luggage and be gone. Nice to see you, brother."

I intended to brush past him and gather more of my luggage.

He stepped in front of me.

"What aren't you telling me?"

If only he knew. A part of me needed him to be the loving brother you see in TV movies. The brother he once was. My eyes teared for the loss of that brother. I wanted him to have my back. The same way his boss had a few minutes before Arie showed him my flaws.

"I've told you everything I know about the situation at the Raymont House. You probably know a lot more than I do. Now, if you'll move, I'll be going home."

'Home,' that house hadn't been home in years, but somehow, it was more of a home than my two-million-dollar apartment in L.A., which wasn't really my apartment. It belonged to my company. When I didn't return from vacation next Monday, they'd be busy packing up my things. But they'd be too late. The movers were already there now. Everything that was mine, which wasn't much, would be in a truck headed to Abracadabra by tonight.

"I can't let you do that."

"You can't let me go to my house?"

He shook his head. "No, you are a person of interest."

And so it begins again. When I got my hands on the serial killer, he was a dead man.

"I have an alibi. Blake already checked." I looked into Arie's face. He would not win this battle.

"Blake, huh? That was before he found out you knew Mr. Raymont. You should have told him."

Really? Come on. I threw up my hands.

"I was twelve. That was decades ago. How is it even relevant? Does he think I went there to settle a forty-year-old score?"

Arie's posture softened a tad. His shoulders rounded a smidge.

"I didn't say you were a suspect. Person of Interest is different."

This was ridiculous. I started around him.

"Look, I can't stay here. This place needs a thorough energy clearing, and I'm not in the right frame of mind to do one this intense today. I promise I won't leave my house. Sampson needs a fenced backyard. We've been on the road for a few days."

He exhaled and ran his hand through his hair.

"Fine. Give me your wallet. I'll follow you to your house, where you'll give me your keys. Do you have dog food for Sampson?"

"Of course, I have food."

"I mean real food for a lab, not woo-woo food for a fussy pixie dog."

Indignation flamed up my body. Yes, I was driving the fancy car and wore expensive clothes, but I was still a Bracken. Cut from the same cloth as my biased brother.

"I may have lived a city life, but I know how to feed a big dog. Whether you choose to believe it or not, the city may have cleaned me up, but you can't wash the country out of me that easily."

He picked up three of my bags with one hand.

"Yeah, right."

"I'm changing the subject to a safer topic," I said, following behind him with my makeup case and carry on. "What happened to Moon Lake? It's lost its vibrancy."

"That is not a safe topic. Not even close."

# CHAPTER 8

Pulling my rented Mercedes into my driveway, I studied the grounds. The white colonial-style house with a wrap-around porch and bay windows stood proudly. Micky, my caretaker, had done an excellent job of keeping the outside of the house and grounds in superb condition. The windows were clean, the yard well-groomed. The perennial beds Grams planted years ago mulched. A white rabbit sat on the porch under the bay window, munching on a twig.

With my makeup case under my arm and my carry-on in my left hand, I unlocked the door and waited for the energy to hit me. Aside from a cardboard and plastic taste in my mouth, the energy felt light and welcoming. Micky had been an excellent caretaker. I needed to write him a note and give him a bonus.

My home was one of the few things I owned. My apartment in L.A. belonged to the company I worked for, as did most of the furnishings and my professional and evening wardrobe.

Today, the few things in my apartment I owned filled one little pod. By now, that pod was on a truck headed this way. There was something solid about walking into a home I owned, free and clear. The inside looked a bit chaotic. Over the years, I gathered items I loved and shipped them here. Most were in the house's two back rooms. A few pieces were scattered throughout the house. A part of me immediately longed to go through them, but I couldn't. I needed to disappear until this whole serial killer thing blew over, and they figured out how my company was connected.

"Faith...Faith...FAITH."

I'd heard him. I was just elsewhere.

"Where do you want me to put these?"

I turned around to see him holding five of my suitcases and Sampson's leash. I'd forgotten about Sampson. He'd been so quiet. The white cat had worn him out. First time since I'd had the pup, he wasn't jumping around like a huge flea.

"Just put them there by the door." I ran my hand over the marble countertop.

"I'd feel better if I put them in the bedroom."

Really, like the location of my bags would keep me here.

"Don't worry. You have my word. I won't rabbit during the night. What's with the lights in Dad's house? Did he rent it to someone?"

He put the bags down in front of the bay window.

"Um, No. He didn't rent it. Dad's back in town. Been back about a month."

Shock tumbled in my solar plexus.

"Mom?"

"She's in and out."

"More in or out?"

"More in. She..." He shook his head.

What was he going to say? Mom probably came in for booty calls. We didn't need to discuss their sex life.

"Just thought I should warn you. The Jasmine Place has occupants on and off, including a mouthy cat and dog. Something tells me Sampson will enjoy himself."

"How is Mr. Jasmine?"

"Long story," was all he said.

"Wow, Abracadabra has gone from ghost town to metropolis in a couple of months."

He stepped in front of me and looked into my eyes.

"What aren't you telling me, Faith?"

At least he didn't bark it out this time. I so wished I could tell him. But he'd only hate me more.

"I'm just anxious to get started on my vacation. My schedule has been packed. The paperwork buries me every night. And on top of that, corporate politics. I'm exhausted."

All of it was true—every word of it.

"I don't believe you, but I won't force it out of you either." He opened the door. "I should tell you. You have a niece. I have a daughter. Her name is Tiffany." He stepped out onto the porch.

What? I had a niece, and no one bothered to tell me.

"Whoa. Hold it right there. Way to bury the lede." The words escaped my mouth.

He stopped and turned, but didn't face me directly.

"Tiffany is seventeen. Anita was her mother." His voice trailed off.

I joined him on the porch. Whoa. My subconscious was processing faster than my conscious.

"What do you mean, was her mother?"

"Anita was murdered two months ago. Tiffany moved in with me. The only reason you didn't meet her today was that she's on a school trip. Won't be back till late tonight."

"How long..." I sat on the porch railing, holding onto a support beam. Wow, this was a lot to process—the poor child. Arie loved Anita with his heart and soul. He had since they'd been kids. But there was always someone else before him in her life.

In high school, he dated Sheryl. And he loved Sheryl deeply. Then she was murdered.

When he started dating Anita again, I was happy for him. Hoped she'd revive the old Arie. But then they weren't dating any longer. No one seemed to know why. I had called to let him know I cared. He never responded.

"I've only known about Tiffany for a couple of months."

"Wasn't Anita married to some big-time restauranteur in Chicago?"

He nodded. "Yes, he was killed, too."

Anguish filled my body. I knew a little about losing my parents. Mine were alive, but they'd been otherwise occupied.

"That poor child." Tears streamed down my cheeks. Something inside me sent me into my brother's arms. I hugged him for the first time in years.

# CHAPTER 9

Bang, bang, bang came from my hotel door. Why? I had the day off. Sampson had jumped off the bed, his toenails clicking against wood floors. Wait. My hotel room didn't have a hardwood floor. The killer found me. A door opened far away.

"Faith, you'd better be here. I know you did not run off and leave Sampson. Even you wouldn't do that."

I came awake. I was home in Abracadabra. The voice belonged to Arie.

"I'm coming up."

"You don't need to do that. Give me a minute." I heard my mouth say. Thankfully, some part of me was awake and rational. Everything came back. Mr. Raymont's body. Arie. His boss. His daughter. What a mess. No vacation.

I threw the covers off. Pain shot up my arm. I couldn't help myself last night. Once Arie was gone, I dug the peanut butter, bread, and jelly out of my carry-on and munched on it and some cookies while I went through the treasures I'd sent home over the years. I'd gone to bed about 4 AM. The wall clock said 7:30 AM. Was it right? Did I know? Did it matter? Less than four hours sleep. How was I supposed to face Attila the Hun?

"You are a Bracken. You'll find a way." Something said to me. What was it? I wasn't sure. Must not be fully conscious. That was it, right?

"Let me get dressed. I'll be right down."

Arie's voice grew softer, but continued. Either he was talking to himself, or someone else was downstairs. At first, I thought it was my traitor dog, but I heard a second voice. Sounded male. Dad maybe. I grabbed a pair of black leggings and a cerulean pullover knee-length sweater and dragged a brush through my long, dark hair. Slipping my feet into my baby pink satin slippers, I ran down the stairs.

Blake stood by the front door. Arie, dressed in jeans and a blue t-shirt with a brown windbreaker, stationed himself at the stairs' bottom. It didn't take my superpower body language reader skills to know they were NOT happy. They'd dug until they found my secret. How should I play this?

"Let me guess. You talked to Harvey," I said, descending the stairs.

"No, we read about him in an FBI file a friend of Captain Bloom's faxed."

Captain Bloom. We were doing formal now. I had wondered how long that would take. Now, I had my answer. They turned as soon as they learned my secret. So much for Family, Love, and Magic.

"I see."

"Do you, Faith?" Arie's eyes narrowed. "Because now Blake's butt is on the line."

Blake crossed his arms.

I couldn't do this without coffee. Oh right. I couldn't go shopping last night because I was under house arrest. I walked over to the sink, pulled a red glass from the cupboard, and drew a glass of fresh well water. Water grounds the spirit. I needed to drink a five-gallon jug.

"So, since you've seen the file, you already know the story."

Blake stepped forward.

"I'd like to hear it from you. Your brother is ready to haul you down to the station and call Special Agent Wallbanger."

"Is this your guys' version of Good Cop, Bad Cop?" I looked from one to the other.

"Faith," Arie's eyes squinted as his voice grew softer.

What the heck. Might as well get this over with.

"Okay, sit down. I'd offer you something, but Arie wouldn't let me have my keys or wallet, so I couldn't stock the cupboards."

"We'll stand," Arie said.

"Fine, suit yourselves." I walked around the couch and sat in my emerald, winged back chair. The sturdiness of the chair gave me strength. I'd taken the plastic off before I went to bed.

Arie and Blake didn't move.

"Six weeks ago, Bonnie—our scheduler—sent me to a home in Hollywood. I drove up and found the homeowner stuck between the bars of the wrought iron fence. Luckily, as was my fate in life, I'd gotten lost, and at the time of the murder, I was on video at a local animal shelter where I'd stopped to ask for directions. The intake specialist at the front counter remembered me because the woman ahead of me thrust her piglet in my arms and raced out the door. I was questioned and released."

"And then what happened?" Blake asked.

"I was dating my immediate supervisor at the time. We went to the Bahamas for two weeks so I could regroup. We came back. I did a couple of consults. No problem. The third consult was in Arizona. As usual, I got lost. I stopped at a trail ride place to ask for directions, and I helped apprehend a runaway horse. I took a picture with the horse and trail boss and arrived at my appointment forty-five minutes late, where I found the homeowner on his marble steps just outside the front door. I called the police. They came. After extensive questioning, they checked my alibi, and I was released."

"Go on," Arie said.

I took a deep breath to try to judge their reactions. Neither of them moved a muscle. I couldn't read them.

"I took another week off, saw a therapist, and then I was sent to our top boss's conservatory. He wanted my opinion on the energy flow in his new edition. I got lost. When I stopped at a farmer's market, I found Samson tied to a pole in a booth. If no one took him, he was going to a kill shelter. How could I resist? I took a picture with the lady who ran the booth. I arrived only fifteen minutes late because they'd told me the appointment was an hour earlier than it had been. The maid told me to go around to the conservatory. I found the owner of our company planted upside down in a banana tree. I called the police. I was taken to the station about three hours later. Special Agent Harvey Wallbanger arrived. He questioned me for hours before releasing me. There have been two more bodies since. Wallbanger calls me every couple of days. He thinks I'm a serial killer. He hasn't said it to my face, but I know he thinks I'm a serial killer."

"Continue," Blake said, looking at his notebook.

"Between Harvey dogging me, the bodies, and my ex-boyfriend supervisor ending our relationship, I had to get away. I intended to do my consult yesterday, swing by here to let Sampson run, and then get on the road to wherever we landed. But instead, I'm here, and you're questioning me like I'm a serial killer and not your sister." I looked into Arie's eyes.

They softened a bit.

"Does that account fit with the details in your file?" I asked, tears flowing down my cheeks. I rubbed my eyes with the sleeve of my sweater.

# CHAPTER 10

"Why didn't you call me after the first body?" Arie raked his hand through his hair.

"And why would I do that?" I didn't want to call you after Raymont Manor, but...

"Because I am your brother and a cop."

I bit the side of my mouth.

"Sure, I'm the screw-up sister who never does anything right and is a flake selling 'snake oil'. I'm going to call my hero cop brother."

"I never called you a screwup." His hands were on his hips, with his feet under them.

"Hah! More times than I can count." I turned my head away. I couldn't stand to look at him.

He dropped onto the couch opposite me.

"Well, you and what you do confuses me. But I would have helped you."

I turned my head back to him. His last comment had cost him something.

"How? You couldn't erase the image from my mind? I had an alibi." My eyes teared. I hadn't cried one tear before I arrived in Abracadabra, and yet here I was, close to tears every minute. "Don't you think I wanted to? I wanted my big cop brother to hug me and tell me everything was all right—that he'd handle it. I thought about it. I called the garden center hoping that a part of the big brother I remembered was inside you, but the machine said you were closed for the day. I left a message."

"We closed the day of Anita's funeral," he almost whispered and paused before continuing. "That doesn't explain the other murders."

"By the time the second body dropped, I'd already been through it once by myself. I'd called. You hadn't responded. I'd been living a long time with no one having my back. Why would I expect or ask for anything different?"

"Had I known, I would have been there. You've never been alone."

Really? It sure felt like it. But looking at my brother now, being in his presence, I knew the hero part of him would have come to my aid.

"Yeah, well, it's in the past. I've handled it. Every time there's been a body, I've had an alibi with pictures, a person, and an animal."

"That doesn't change things." Arie raked his hand through his dark hair again. By the time we ended this conversation, he would be bald.

"If I may interject," Blake said. He left the doorway where he'd been standing and took a seat on the light pink couch next to Arie.

"While you have a legitimate alibi and aren't a murder suspect, I've got to wonder how and why someone picks your consultations to drop bodies, as you put it."

I took a breath. Him saying 'I wasn't a suspect' were words I needed to hear.

"Trust me, that thought has crossed my mind. That's why I planned to disappear. My apartment is packed, and on a truck, headed here. Micky promised to meet the driver and unload my stuff into the spare bedroom."

For just a second, it felt good to sit in a chair I owned, in a house I owned, on property I owned. Surrounded by land, my family—no matter how estranged we were—held. For a second, the ground beneath me felt stable. And then I remembered Special Agent Harvey Wallbanger.

"Did one of you call Harvey?"

"You've talked to him that many times you call him by his first name?" Blake asked, leaning back on the couch.

"No, I just refer to him as Harvey, so he isn't so scary."

Blake looked at Arie. Arie shook his head.

"You've not called him yet?" I could hardly believe what I was hearing. I figured Harvey would be pulling in any minute.

"No, not yet," Blake said. "I should have called him this morning. But I wanted to talk to you first."

I caught Blake's eyes.

"Thank You. You've been nothing but kind."

Arie huffed at that statement.

"Blake's butt will be in deep trouble if he doesn't call Special Agent Wallbanger." Arie snickered as he said the words. He tried to gloss over his slip.

"See, as mad as you are, you can't keep a straight face and say his name."

For just a second, the Arie I remembered from our childhood appeared, and then he was gone. I would miss that look.

I leaned across the arm of my chair, reaching for the drawer in the end table. Blake tensed. His hand moved towards his gun. Arie's eyes grew wide. They didn't think I would pull out a gun. Did they?

I retrieved my all-time favorite deck of oracle cards. I'd missed this deck. Not quite sure how I knew it was in the drawer, but I did. Shuffling, I said a silent prayer as I concentrated on the image on the back of the cards—silently asking for guidance. After shuffling eleven times, I pulled a card. Arie's eyes rolled. He hated woo-woo. I flipped the card over.

# CHAPTER 11

A face and a bear appeared on the card.

"I'll be right back."

The two men exchanged looks. Arie shrugged.

I ran up the stairs and returned with my phone.

Flipping through my contacts, I found the number I needed. Putting it on speaker, I waited for him to answer.

"Special Agent Wallbanger."

"It's Faith Bracken. I found another body last night." Except for the sound of a page flipping, there was a moment of silence.

"I'm glad you called, Ms. Bracken. My system alerted me a few moments ago. Someone ran your name. Stay where you are. I'll be there in two hours."

"I'll be here." I gave him my address. My gut clenched while waves of terror and bleakness fought inside me. Could I deal with Harvey again? Not really. But this time, perhaps I had backup.

Blake touched my hand.

"Thank you. You did the right thing."

*I sure hope so.*

Arie went to the backdoor to let Sampson out.

"When is your moving truck arriving?" he asked on his way back.

"Friday."

"While I'm waiting for the FBI, is there anything you need moved?"

Blake stood.

"Yeah, while we wait, we might as well do something constructive."

Wow, I didn't see that one coming. So like Arie. When it comes to emotional family stuff, Arie works instead. *Let him off the hook, Faith.*

"You two don't have to be here. I can handle Harvey by myself." Not that I wanted to, but I had experience.

"Technically, you are a person of interest. We would be derelict in our duties if we left you alone," said Blake.

"And moving furniture is part of your job description."

He shrugged. "We need to stay fit."

"Oh, trust me, we'll get our workout," Arie said. "She's a drill sergeant. I once spent ten hours moving furniture from one place to another and back over and over and over again."

"Is that true?" Blake asked, smiling at me.

"How do you think he passed the endurance test to get accepted into the police academy?"

"Not true," Arie said.

They followed me into the room where Micky had stored most of the treasures I'd sent home.

"So, this bed frame and mattress need to go upstairs."

Yes, it was king size. They were tough. It'd be good for them—only one flight of narrow stairs.

Arie looked at the mattress and then at me. "Of course it does."

"You offered, Bro."

"Me and my big mouth." He moved a desk from in front of the headboard.

"Come on, you two big strong men can handle this with no problem."

Blake smirked as he picked up one end of the king-sized mattress.

"Notice she didn't add handsome to that statement."

Arie grabbed the other end.

"Do not encourage her."

Fifteen minutes later, I fished around in Grams' old tool drawer and found an Allen wrench.

"I thought simplicity was part of your Zen. This thing must have a hundred pieces," Blake said, flipping the wrench up and over several times.

I sat on the floor cross-legged and gave directions.

"Our motto is to surround yourself with the things you love. It was love at first sight for me. I bought it at an estate sale the day after I moved to Los Angeles." My voice trailed off, thinking of Grams' funeral. I left the night we buried her.

"Speaking of moving. What the heck happened to Moon Lake?"

The two guys looked at each other.

"There's been a feud between the people who live in the township and those who live in the town. And between the residents who live in Abracadabra and those who live in Moon Lake."

"Over?" I handed them another screw.

"The people in the town wanted a state-of-the-art new school. The way property taxes are structured, the people who live in the unincorporated part of the township would bear the burden of paying for it. Moon Lake tried to annex Abracadabra, but Vito hired a fancy lawyer and got that idea nixed."

Dad getting involved in local politics. Dad back in Abracadabra. Something was wrong. Should I ask? Or wait for them to tell me?

"But Moon Lake has always been a rich little town."

"It was until everyone got their tail feathers twisted," Arie said. "Several businesses have closed. It's not a nice place to be right now."

"But," Blake said, tightening a screw. "Moon Lake has a new part-time mayor who is trying to heal the divide."

"Did they get the new school?"

"No, the people in the county won," Blake said.

"Did they need a new school?"

Arie shoved a slat into place.

"Our old school needs an upgrade. The faction pushing for a new school went overboard. It had to be their way or no way. Heated arguments turned into physical altercations."

Moon Lake had always been a mystical, prosperous little village. Lots of interconnected families. My mind struggled to form an image.

"In Moon Lake?"

"Yep, do you think we'd lie to you?"

No, I knew Arie wasn't a liar. As that thought formed and followed. I realized for the first time in weeks my anxiety meter was down a point. I'd gone from fifteen to fourteen. Maybe even thirteen point five.

# CHAPTER 12

Sampson, who'd been actively sniffing every inch of thawing mud and grass in his backyard, ran from the back corner to the screen door, pawing for all his little body was worth.

"Looks like The Fed is here," Blake said from the other room where he'd gone at Sampson's alert. "Sampson shows potential as a watchdog."

If I was going to keep Sampson—and how could I not—Sampson needed doggie school. That meant staying in one place long enough for him to graduate. Geez! I sounded like a parent.

Just nerves.

I took a deep breath and rose to my feet, using the bed frame to steady myself. It held. They'd done an excellent job. Arie had already gone downstairs. As I descended the stairs, I heard Blake open the front door and join Arie on the front porch. I needed another deep breath. I could do this—one more breath.

"You've got this, Faith." I heard a voice say. Great, now I'm talking to myself and don't even know I'm doing it.

I walked onto the porch to find the three men sitting in chairs. When had the chairs arrived? They weren't there last night. My face must have registered my shock. Arie mouthed the word "Dad." That was so like Vito. He came in the middle of the night. Altered your world and disappeared. Kind of like a round, pint-sized mob boss, Lone Ranger.

Harvey stood to shake my hand.

"Ms. Bracken, it's good to see you. Thank you for contacting me."

"You would have found out anyhow."

He smiled. "I've noticed you don't mince words, do you?"

I moved a can of instant coffee off one of the chairs and pulled it slightly away from the others towards the steps. Vito thought of everything.

"I assume you want me to tell you about finding Mr. Raymont's body?"

He took his phone out and pushed the record button. "If you don't mind."

I proceeded to tell him the entire story.

"I understand you knew the victim."

"I did. I met his daughter at art camp when we were seven. We became best friends. I spent several weekends at Raymont Manor until Lizzie moved to live with her mother in New York. We were both twelve. I had not returned to Raymont Manor until yesterday."

"Are you still in contact with Lizzie?"

"On Social Media. I read her posts from time to time. I'm sure she reads mine. We are casual acquaintances. Lizzie's new stepdad was the head of a hedge fund. My father was rumored to be a Vegas Crime Boss. Not really the same circles."

"Your father is Vito Bracken."

"He is." Arie crossed his arms. Dad's "occupation" had always been a sore spot for Arie. I believed Arie joined the military to get away from the stigma of being Vito Bracken's son, as well as the pain of losing Sheryl.

"When was Raymont Manor added to your schedule? By whom?"

"Bonnie, our scheduler, called me late afternoon the day before. She wanted me to do a consult in Chicago, and then I was free to start my vacation. She suggested I complete Mr. Raymont's home and then take the train from Michigan City to Chicago. I said no. I'd take Raymont Manor and then start my vacation. She hissed but finally agreed to send someone else."

"Why didn't you want to take the consult in Chicago? Did you have a plane to catch?"

He was trying to see if I was skipping the country again. I didn't skip last time. I was sent.

"No. Since I was so close to home, I wanted to bring Sampson here to play in his backyard."

"How much money do you make off each consultation?"

Indignation threatened to blow my cool, but he most likely already knew the answer.

"$10,000 per consultation." I watched Blake and Arie's eyes grow wide in surprise.

"And yet you passed up $10,000 to bring your puppy home to play in his pen?"

When he put it like that, my plan sounded ridiculous. How could I explain? At some point, my sanity trumped money.

"What I do is part art, part science, and part spirit. The art and spirit parts are drained. I needed time to replenish them."

"And you didn't have one more consultation in you."

No, I'd vomit if I had to do another consultation for Crescent, but I wasn't going to tell him that.

"I needed rest more than I needed the money."

"Aren't you, in fact, a high-class hooker, Faith?"

So, he'd finally said what I'd known he'd been thinking. Before I could say a word, Arie jumped to his feet. Harvey remained seated. Blake stood next to Arie.

"You need to leave," Arie said. Every muscle in his body tensed, preparing for a beat down.

"It's okay, Arie," I placed my hand on my brother's arm. "I've got this. So, you finally said it. I'm curious why you waited to accuse me of being a hooker until I was seated in front of my cop brother and his captain. You've been thinking it since day one."

"Am I thinking it because it is true?"

Arie clenched his fists.

"He's not worth it," Blake said.

"No. It is not true. Feng Shui is an ancient art form. I do not touch my clients. And before you ask. No jealous boyfriend is killing them either. I'm on the road 360 days a year. Sure, I dated my supervisor for a short time, but it was only a minute, and he broke it off because I was gone constantly, and dead bodies met me at the door. Not good for his image."

"So, how do you plan to take care of a dog if you are on the road 360 days a year?"

"I didn't know the FBI had a doggie unit," Blake said. "Unless you have more questions about Mr. Raymont's murder, I think we are finished here."

Harvey put his phone in his pocket.

"I don't at this time. Don't leave town, Faith." He walked toward his car.

# CHAPTER 13

Just when I was about to breathe, Harvey turned around.

"We're taking over the Raymont investigation. Captain Bloom, you'll have paperwork within the hour."

"How long have you been dealing with that jerk?" Blake asked as Harvey shut his door.

"Since the murder of the owner of my company a few weeks ago. And for the record, I have never slept with nor had sexual relations of any kind with my clients. Most I never see. They fill out a form. A domestic helper grants me access to the home. I write my reports, and Brittany, our office manager, sets an appointment with one of our sales representatives to discuss the report and implement my suggestions. I seldom have direct contact. If a client wishes to purchase any of the items suggested in my report, they are directed to a sales representative. Maybe once a quarter, a client insists on meeting me, and then I am always accompanied by a sales representative."

"So, if you seldom meet your clients, why does your company pay for your car, clothes, etc.?" Arie asked.

"As I said, part of what I do is art, part science, and part spiritual. Our clients are the top one percent. We, as consultants, need to move in that lifestyle to understand

them. They all have video systems. Can't have us show-
ing up in five-dollar jeans and a t-shirt."

"But none of the murders are captured on video."
Blake opened the door and escorted me inside. I just
realized it was cold.

"Weird, I know. I've thought of that too."

"So, how many consultations a week do you have?"
Blake asked.

"Sometimes as many as twenty. I'm the busiest consultant because I can do homes, businesses, and farms.
My specialty is gardens."

"Makes sense," Arie said. "Given you grew up between
a Montana Ranch and an Indiana Garden Center."

"Our Aunt Georgia owns one of the premier home
furnishing brands," I said to Blake as I set the can of
coffee on the counter.

"Does your company carry your aunt's line?"

I shook my head and drew a glass of water.

"Sadly, no. My aunt isn't a fan of my company. I'm not
sure why. "

"Do you get a commission on the items sold by your
company?"

What was he trying to do? Figure out if I was a hit-
woman for hire.

"No. Some consultants do. I was afraid it would cloud
my judgment. As I said, part of what I do is spiritual. I
try to keep my energy pure."

Sampson trotted over and pawed me until I petted
him.

"And yet you find yourself tripping over dead bodies,"
Blake said.

I walked into the living room and sat down.

"I know. I have meditated and done all the spiritual fixes I know. I've not found an answer."

Blake's phone buzzed. "Got the fed's paperwork. That was fast."

Arie grabbed a cup of coffee from the microwave and sat on a stool at the counter.

"I don't care. Someone is dropping bodies for my sister to find. This is personal. Harvey wants to make Faith guilty. Not going to happen."

So, whose honor was Arie defending mine or his? Deep down. I knew he was protecting his little sister. Whether or not the woman in front of him was still considered his sister remained to be seen. The last thing I wanted was to create more drama with my family. He didn't need to fight my battles.

"Arie, I've seen enough TV. You go up against the Feds, and your career could be ruined. You already have a questionable father. Just let me disappear. I am sure this is about my company. Someone is trying to bring them down. If I disappear, whoever is doing it will have to pick another consultant to harass. It will prove it's about my company and not me."

"Faith," Blake leaned forward in his chair, "Rather than disappear since you are always on the road, why don't you work out a deal to work from Abracadabra? Tell them you need a few weeks off to give the police time to find the killer. Can you afford to take a few weeks off? They aren't going to drop bodies under the nose of two cops and a mob boss."

"Arie didn't tell me you lived in Abracadabra."

"I do, now."

H'm. What exactly did the 'now' mean?

"Okay, first off. No matter what Arie might have told you. I do not squander money. I socked away most of what I've made taxes didn't eat up. Second, I don't need you two to protect me. I've been doing that all by myself for a long time."

"And look where that got you," Arie said.

See, he could only be nice to me for so long. I knew mean Arie would come out again soon.

"So, you think I did something to cause this?"

Arie raked his hand through his hair.

"I didn't say that."

No, but it's in your body language.

"You know that irritates me when you read my body language. It always has and will."

"Sorry for being me." I turned to talk to Blake. "The only way I'm staying is if you promise to help me figure out who killed Mr. Raymont. I didn't tell Harvey, but this murder is different."

Arie raked his hand through his hair again. The thick black hair flopped back into place from too much practice. He really needed new gestures. I could read him like a book.

"Different how?" Arie asked. "And you couldn't have told us that sooner?"

"I didn't realize it until I talked to Harvey, and I'm not used to sharing."

"Faith, we need you to trust us," Blake said. "Different how?"

How much should I tell them? I needed to choose my words carefully, or Arie would be hopping mad.

"Well, Mr. Raymont was hidden away. All the others have been out in the open where I couldn't miss the bodies.

And the bodies have been posed. Mr. Raymont just fell out." It sounded horrible when I said it. "Third, every other murder victim has had a picture of me with my full name scribbled across it and a bag of little bones. Mr. Raymont didn't. There was a message on the first body."

Blake's arm rested on my shoulder.

"Faith, what was the message?"

"You must clear your demons before you plant your dreams."

Arie crossed to the living room and grabbed me by both shoulders.

"What demons, Faith?"

"All my demons are related to Abracadabra and family. Since I left here, I've been on the road constantly."

Arie's eyes clouded, and his mouth fell open. I felt his hold soften.

"I thought you said your company doesn't use your last name," Blake said, changing the subject.

"They don't. And they certainly don't use my middle name. I've grabbed the pictures and the bones out of the victim's hands every time before I called the police."

This time, both guys raked their hands through their hair. I would have to get out the vacuum to suck up the stray hairs.

"Why?"

"Why were the pictures and bones there? Or why did I take it from their hands?"

"I don't know. Both," said Arie.

"Why and how they have a picture of me with my full name? I have no idea. Why I took it from their hands has to do with my spiritual beliefs."

Arie began pacing. If I stuck around too long, he'd be skin and bones.

"So, what do the bones mean to your spiritual beliefs?"

"Bones can represent several things."

Blake touched my hand. His was warm and comforting.

"What do they mean to you, Faith? The killer is leaving them with your picture and full name."

"Bones to me, mean areas of your life left unfed, not nurtured."

"So, what would those areas be for you, Faith?" Blake asked.

"Wow, talk about feeling vulnerable."

I am sorry, but if we are going to help, we need to understand. This killer has chosen you for a reason. Knowing your answers could lead us to the killer. And clear this madness out of your life."

Madness exactly captured my world these last few weeks. Blake exuded empathy.

"Well, my family. As I'm sure you noticed, we have issues. And I guess my home. I mean, I own a house here, but I live on the road. I wasn't seriously dating anyone. And career-wise, I wanted a change."

Blake looked from Arie to me.

"Roll with me here. Have you seen anyone recently following you that looks vaguely familiar from Abracadabra? Unusual contact with someone connected to Abracadabra or your family?"

I shook my head. "No."

Blake and Arie looked at each other again. I imagined silent thoughts beaming from one to the other.

"Is there anyone in your past you dated who thought you were more serious than you did?" Arie asked.

"Well, it's hard to know another's thoughts."

"Yeah, but with your body language skills...."

"No one I can think of. I haven't exaggerated. I am always on the road. Sometimes I do three cities in one day."

"The pictures. Do you have them? Are they the same picture or different? Are they marketing photos or candid?" Arie asked.

"They are in my carry-on. The first one was from a marketing brochure. The others have been from the previous crime scene."

"Faith, we need to see those photos." Blake made notes in a little book.

"Somehow, I figured that." Walking back into the kitchen, I opened my carry-on parked in the corner and retrieved the photos inside the pouch marked dog treats. I handed them and the bones to Arie."

He grabbed a tissue and flipped through them. His muscles tightened. I couldn't tell if he was mad at me for withholding evidence from the police or at the killer. He handed them off to Blake.

"We need to run these for prints."

"Won't that alert Harvey."

Blake flipped his notebook closed.

"You let me worry about Harvey. Back to your company. If you disappear but can stay plugged into the investigation, you're waiting to see what happens to the bones and pictures," Blake surmised. "That's an Arie move."

Arie glared at Blake.

"The problem with your plan is if you disappear and someone is after you or wants to hurt Vito, you've made yourself an easy target," said Arie. "No one would know you're missing."

So, he'd said what I'd been wondering.

"Yeah, I thought this might be about Vito too," I admitted, dropping onto a stool. We'd always be marked by our father's reputation.

"You need to stay here. I'll be right back." Blake opened the front door and stepped onto the porch. From the window, I watched him go to his car and retrieve a phone. "Call your company and tell them we are holding you for your protection."

"I can't. A courier is delivering my resignation as we speak. I set it up before I left."

Arie shook his head.

"When are you going to trust me?"

"Working on it. I've been alone a long time. Talking about trust, you still have my keys and wallet."

He looked into my eyes.

"I want you to hear this. You were never alone. Just too stubborn to call." He pulled my keys out of his pocket and threw them to me. "Your wallet is locked in your car."

"Thank You."

"Don't leave, Faith. There's more you need to know."

# CHAPTER 14

A few minutes later, Arie and Blake were called to another assignment. The house immediately felt empty. The two of them took up a lot of space. They also made me feel safe and distracted me from the decision I needed to make. Either I stayed here, or I left and disappeared.

Leaving was easy. Staying meant feeding the oldest dried bone. Was I ready for messy?

Arie was as nice as Arie could be because no one messed with his family, but sooner or later, his dislike of everything I was would reappear.

Vito was already on the scene. Family was messy. Especially our family. And Arie had a "new" daughter. A daughter who'd lost both the parents she knew, and now she had Arie. Emotionally distant Arie. Arie who thought feelings were worse than criminals. Poor kid.

But it wasn't my place to be a mother for his daughter. I could be an aunt. Would Arie even let me near his daughter? Staying and dealing with the family was scarier than a crazed killer. No. Two crazed killers. The serial killer and Mr. Raymont's murderer.

But I had Sampson to think of now. We'd only been home a few hours, and already he was in love with his pen. I'd seen a flyer for a pet store opening in

Abracadabra—which was a strange place to open a pet store—when I was inside Arie's house. It had been ages since Abracadabra was a town. From what I could tell, the pet shop didn't appear to be open yet, but I thought I'd seen a website. If we stayed, helping the local businesses would be an excellent start to lay roots. Funny, Arie hadn't mentioned a new business opening in town. Maybe that was part of the "more I needed to know."

Sampson did love it here. And I fully believed a pet was a lifetime commitment. Of course, if a serial killer was after me, my lifetime wasn't very long, and Sampson was in the line of fire.

I needed these murders behind me. Running away and disappearing didn't seem like the solution, no matter how easy it seemed. So next question. If I stayed, what would I do with myself? I could start my own Feng Shui company. I'd signed a non-compete to not work within two hundred miles of Los Angeles, but I was hundreds of miles away, so no problem. I'd be starting from scratch. There was nothing to stop me from using my former employer's name in my biography.

Sampson's care meant I couldn't travel as I had. I wouldn't be able to charge my former employer's prices, but I didn't need the money. I had socked away a tidy sum over the years. My home was paid for. So, my living expenses were taxes, food, clothes, utilities, toys for Sampson, and a vehicle. Not zero, but not impossible.

However, I had a better idea. I wanted to start a Flower Farm. I needed to use a few acres of my land, and I needed some help.

So much to think about. Time for a walk and a trip to the grocery store.

# CHAPTER 15

Sampson must read minds because the minute I rose from my chair, he hopped out of his bed, crossed the room, and tugged his leash from the hook.

"That's right, Sampson. It's time for a walk." By the time I slipped into my boots, placed my phone in my jacket pocket, and pulled on my mittens, he was seated in front of the door, willing it to open. I grabbed the leash loop and turned the doorknob. The air was crispy but not intolerable. We were off on today's adventure.

The Flower Farm was in the hazy wave stage in my mind. I thought it was a great idea, and I had some plans, but I needed to work out all the other details. Which piece of property would be best? Zoning? Taxes? Water supply? Building codes? Access? Traffic flow? Should I start this season or wait until next? What would season one look like? Goals for season two? What metrics would I use for success? How would I advertise and market my business? Should I add a floral shop? The one in Abracadabra had closed last month. The physical shop wasn't in the best place. There wasn't a shop in Moon Lake. The closest were either Plymouth, South Bend, or North Liberty. Did I want to run a floral shop? I'd have to hire staff. If I

opened The Flower Farm, how would I run my Feng Shui
Practice?

I'd heard Aunt Georgia was thinking of closing the in-
terior decor showroom. How would or could that fit into
The Floral Farm and my consultations? I never saw my
apartment in L.A. because I was on the road constantly.
If I stayed, and for Sampson's sake, I was leaning in that
direction, did I want to work as much? I wanted to live in
my home, furnished with my taste, surrounded by things I
loved. Would it be that much different from the constant
travel if I worked twenty-four-seven? Probably not. The
only difference was my wardrobe would stay in the same
closet, and I'd have to dust and cook.

Most of the property in Abracadabra belonged to the
Bracken Family Trust. I owned a piece of that property.
We'd never decided which property belonged to whom.
Nothing Fancy technically belonged to all of us, but it was
Arie's to handle as he saw fit in practice. I had my choice.
Where would I put The Flower Farm? The smartest thing
for me to do was take over Aunt Georgia's shop and run
my Feng Shui Business out of her storefront.

But a Flower Farm was my dream. Creating it in my
mind got me through the last few weeks. The idea had
been calling me since I performed a consultation for a
flower farm on the West Coast. That day, I stood on the
Pacific Coast, and yet I stood in Abracadabra at the same
time. It had been the weirdest of the weird experiences in
my life. And I knew 'weird.'

Sampson yanked on his chain, pulling me from my
thoughts. A black and white rabbit darted inches in front
of Sampson and ran around him. Sampson, who was teth-
ered to me, wasn't happy. He wanted to chase his new

friend. He lunged, pulling me with him. I knew he wanted to run, but he hadn't yet been adequately trained. He took off. I had no choice. I did my best to keep up. The rabbit zigged and zagged. It would stop, peek from behind a tree, and zip off again. The crazy little critter was fast. It stopped in front of a mugo pine, watched us, made sure we followed him, and darted towards a clump of dead weeds. Did it want us to follow it? Sometimes when animals are hurt, another animal will instinctively know humans can help. Was that happening now? Or was it leading me to my doom?

We must have followed that rabbit for fifteen minutes before it disappeared behind a rock not far from the old magic factory.

When Abracadabra deserved a place on the map, The Abracadabra Magic Factory had been the anchor of Abracadabra. Today, it was an abandoned factory consisting of one grand brick building, two smaller brick buildings, and several pole barns. Sampson and I stood at the mouth of the lane, which led into the factory grounds. A little rabbit popping out of a hat statue pointed traffic toward the factory. I guessed it was fitting the rabbit led us here.

I'd forgotten how beautiful this piece of ground to the south of the factory was. A creek wound in a meandering path to a large pond further south. The Bracken Family Trust paid taxes on the old factory. Perhaps it was time to get some use out of the building and combine the floral shop and flower farm into one spot. Although heating the main building would be astronomical. But it was a thought. And today was about ideas.

I believed in a good plan, but I had also learned that true inspiration came while doing the work. Today I was doing the work and getting the feel. Thinking. This piece of land felt right. The urge to take my shoes off and soak up the energy emanating from the earth overwhelmed my senses, but it was cold, and the ground was slightly frozen. My feet would not be happy if I succumbed to my urges.

"This spot is perfect," a voice said.

I jumped. Sampson didn't move. So much for him being a watchdog.

"What the heck?" I turned in a circle. No one seemed to be anywhere.

"You are not crazy," the voice said. "You just aren't ready to see me."

Not sure a disembodied voice was the best judge of my mental health.

"Who or what are you?"

"I'm a Lighter," it said. Okay, now inanimate objects were talking to me. Did it want me to build a fire?

"Like a Bic?" What a stupid question. But what does one say to a voice without a body?

"No, think witch, ghost, or alchemist 5.0."

Yeah, right? Not crazy. Sure! I couldn't get a read. Was it male or female? The voice was thin and high, but not squeaky.

"I don't think I can think that. What do you want?"

"In good time, my dear. In good time."

That wasn't an answer. I couldn't even comprehend.

"If you aren't going to tell me what you want, why did you speak to me?"

"You're a thinker, aren't you? Well, I wanted to tell you, you are right where the grand plan needs you to be. I want you to notice those times when you are in the in-between."

My legs felt shaky. My brain had to be playing tricks on me. That was the only explanation. I needed to get back. I needed real food. I needed to go grocery shopping. I needed to get away from this spot and regain my sanity.

"It won't work," the voice said. "You can't run. You've been doing that for a very long time. You need to heal those demons of yours before you can plant your dreams."

OMG. That comment stopped me in my tracks. I spun around again, attempting to find the location of the voice—that phrase.

I didn't tell Arie and Blake the note left with the first body was written on notebook paper. When I picked it up, it disappeared in my hand. At the time, I thought it was made of acid, and I'd probably lose my hand. Instead, nothing happened. Except now, I was crazy.

"You are not crazy. Stop thinking that. You have more important work to do."

Sampson and the little bunny sat there listening, almost as if they understood.

"But you aren't going to tell me what work." Where was the voice coming from? I couldn't get a fix on it. It was sometimes all around me and sometimes in one place.

"I just did. Notice when you enter the in-between."

"And I told you I don't know what that is."

"Yes, you do. I'll expect you to explain it to me in a few days. Think of it as your homework."

"Did you kill those men?" I asked. Until an hour ago, when I told Arie and Blake, no one knew about the phrase. Did someone have my house or phone bugged?

"No, I did not. I merely used the killer's actions to push you along your path. Do your homework." I wasn't sure if I felt or experienced a whoosh. The presence was gone.

I glanced at Sampson. He sat on my right foot, staring in the direction the voice had last been.

"Sampson, I wish you could talk. It would be nice to know you heard the voice, too."

"If I said I did. You'd think you were crazy talking to a dog." I heard Sampson think. He was right. I was only more freaked—time to get some groceries. We jogged back to the house and headed for the grocery store. I could not process this. It didn't happen. It didn't happen. It sooo didn't happen.

# CHAPTER 16

It was after 6 pm. I was just about to fix a sandwich from the bags of groceries on the counter when Sampson chased from the living room to the kitchen, into the open pantry door, and back towards the front door. The sound of car doors slamming renewed my faith in Sampson's future as a watchdog. It was nice to know his antics weren't a message to feed him. I was still learning to speak Sampson. I found myself hoping the car belonged to Blake.

It wasn't. Parked in my driveway was a Prius. Lizzie Raymont Makey and her husband stomped towards the house. Charles yelled into his phone. As they grew closer, I determined the target of his ire was the car rental company. My guess is Charles thought the Prius was not up to his standards. Lizzie looked old and tired. Her internal vibrancy gone. Of course, she'd just lost her father. I went onto the porch to greet my old friend.

Stepping through the door, I opened my arms to hug her on the porch. Lizzie immediately backed up. Charles towered over me. Sampson pushed his way between us and sat on my foot. Hurt by her rebuke, I took a beat to regroup.

"Lizzie, I am so sorry. Your father was such a dear man."

"How could you?" she said. "My father bent over backward for you. There were times I thought he loved you more than he loved me. How could you do it to him?"

Sampson growled, and I reached down to pick him up. Holding him gave me an excuse to hug myself.

"I don't... I don't... I don't understand." The words seemed stuck in my mouth. Sadness weighed down on me.

"Someone is killing your clients, and you led them straight to my father. Why? Why, Faith? Why would you do that?"

Sampson growled louder—most likely because I was squeezing him. I didn't know what to say, do, or feel. Numbness was all I had to offer.

"Would you like to sit down?" I motioned to the living room. "I just moved home last night. The groceries are still in bags, or I'd offer you something."

"We don't want anything but an explanation." Lizzie's voice trailed off into tears. Her body shook. I wanted to comfort my friend, but what could I do?

"Lizzie, we were friends. I loved your family. What makes you think I'd put your dad in harm's way?"

"When everyone around you ends up dead, there has to be something wrong with you," she said, shredding a tissue.

Anger like I had never known shot up my body. My presence shook.

"If you believe that, what are you doing here?" Immediately, I regretted my words.

"There are two of us, and you wouldn't kill us on your own property," Charles said.

So, he thought I was a serial killer. Even if the bodies stopped dropping, and despite the fact I always had an alibi, this case would haunt me forever unless the real killer was convicted.

"Are you sure about that?"

As soon as I'd asked that question, I felt even worse. What was up with my mouth? Lizzie had just lost her father. Mr. Raymont was a larger-than-life character. As strange as my parents were, I knew I was lucky they were both alive.

"Are you threatening us?" Charles said.

I hung my head.

"Of course not. Lizzie and I are friends. Look, I didn't know I was doing a consultation for your dad until the night before. The murders happened on the West Coast. I don't know why I am the one to always trip over the body, but I am. That doesn't mean he's killing because of me. Often, Bonnie assigns clients at the last minute. It's not like I have time to plan their murders.

Charles's phone dinged. He grabbed Lizzie's elbow and hauled her towards the door.

"Time to go."

"Lizzie, please believe me. I am so sorry." She looked at me and then turned and allowed Charles to drag her to the car.

# CHAPTER 17

Even though it was cold, I sat on the porch for a while. The crisp fresh air felt calming after the drama. I wanted to sit there forever, but I remembered the frozen food in the grocery bags. On some level, I must have decided to stay in Abracadabra because there was enough food in these bags to feed ten Pro-Football teams. Ten! And it took three times longer to put things away because I constantly needed to stop and dry my eyes with a paper towel. Good thing I'd packed those on top.

How in the world could Lizzie think I intentionally had anything to do with her father's murder? And then another difference between Mr. Raymont's death and the other murders hit me. All the others had been on my schedule a few days in advance. The times and cities were blocked out on my calendar several days prior. Mr. Raymont had been a last-minute addition. It wasn't uncommon. It made sense if one of us was going to be in the area to add another client to our calendar, but all the deaths had been on my calendar at least a week before. That was a lead, right?

Who should I tell? Harvey had been a jerk, and I wasn't sure whose side he was on. Arie and Blake could get into big trouble if they meddled. So, who should I tell? It was time to place a call to Blister. Blister, I knew I could trust.

He picked up on the first ring.

"Hey, Lazy Butt, you are the talk of the office."

"Have they sent a team to clear my apartment?"

"Of course, and they found you'd already up and left. Junior is flipping mad, and I do mean flipping. Fire came out of his ears, nostrils, and mouth at the same darn time. Most entertaining day we've ever had here in sunny California."

"Well, I'm glad I could add some excitement to your work life. I need some help."

"Sure thing, Sexy Bottom. Tell me whatcha need."

"I'm going to give you a few dates and times. Can you tell me when the appointments were actually made?"

"Girl, you know I can. If Bonnie did her job correctly, I could tell you almost anything you want to know. I'll hit you back when I have your answer."

"You are my favorite man."

"Don't I know it, darling? On a serious side, you okay?"

"Yes. I think I am. I loved my job, but I think I'll be happy moving on."

"Catch you later, My Queen."

"Bye, Blister."

I realized I hadn't lied. It was time for me to put on my big girl underwear and explore the maze of complications that was and is my family. If the serial killer was going to take me out. I wanted to be at peace with my family, no matter how screwed up they were. I also wanted to be at peace with my best childhood friend.

Lizzie was hurt. She didn't really believe I killed or had anything to do with her father's death. The way we left things made me feel horrible.

# CHAPTER 18

I sat on the couch and wrapped myself in an Alpaca throw. I didn't usually splurge, but this throw had been a splurge well worth it. I'd sent it home after I'd bought it. I'd been waiting a long time for this moment. Too bad I couldn't fully enjoy it.

One good thing about Lizzie's visit, I had momentarily forgotten about the strange encounter on my earlier walk. I told myself it didn't happen. But I knew it did. And I had a hunch I knew what the voice was talking about when it said The In-between.

As a high schooler, the band director used to say the music happens between the beats. I never really understood what he meant until I started to practice Feng Shui. I learned from experience that a nanosecond after opening a door, a void existed before the building's energy hit me. There was another nanosecond before I named the energy. Others didn't seem to notice, but I felt it. The more I practiced, the more notable and longer I was in the energy, but not the physical room.

A wise set designer who worked in my aunt's store told me once, "I know the vignette is correct when I feel a brush of peace."

I didn't understand her either, but her comment haunted me. I researched and found Feng Shui, and the rest, as they say, is history. Over the years, I'd come to understand what she meant. It's in those voids where magic slips in.

So why did I need to notice it? I worked with it almost every day.

And why was I even having this discussion with myself? Because while I wanted to write the incident off as temporary insanity, I knew I couldn't. I knew it happened. I knew it was real. I knew I'd been called home for a reason. And while I'd like to think that reason was to start a flower farm, I sensed it was more. Much more.

"All will be revealed in good time," said the voice. "Rest now. You've been through a great deal."

# CHAPTER 19

Despite my day yesterday and spending my night on the couch, I'd slept like a baby. When I awoke, I knew what I needed to do.

I needed to call Lizzie. I could not stand the way we left things. We'd been best friends. You don't let that kind of friendship go sour. It's not good for the energy of the cosmos. Take a deep breath and call Lizzie. You can do this.

On the other hand. Why was I such a wimp lately with this deep scared of everything sort of persona? Like my brain had to push away the anxiety to think. Every time another body dropped, it got harder and harder to think. What the heck was wrong with me?

But it didn't matter right now. Right now, the only thing I needed to think about was calling Lizzie. I could contact her through social media. But I wanted to talk to her voice to voice and face to face. Did the phone at Raymont Manor still work? Were Lizzie and Charles staying there? There was only one way to find out. Strange, in my new reality, I couldn't remember if I took my morning vitamins, but I could remember the phone number for Raymont Manor.

Pulling out my phone, I dialed the same number I'd called daily as a tween. Back then, I used a rotary phone. Lizzie, to my surprise, answered on the second ring.

"Lizzie, don't hang up. It's Faith."

"Yes," Lizzie said in a broken voice. At least she was talking to me.

"Lizzie, I feel terrible about the way we left things." Before I had the last word out of my mouth, she answered.

"I know. Me too."

"Do you suppose we could have lunch and talk? We are friends. We were best friends. I want to be there for you." I crossed my fingers and waited.

It was quiet on the other end for a few moments. Should I go on talking or wait? Finally, Lizzie responded.

"Charles has an appointment in Chicago this afternoon. I don't suppose there is a Bonnie Doon Restaurant around anymore?"

I laughed. "No, sorry, I already checked. I so wanted one of their burgers last night."

"Me too. How about Doc's at 1pm?"

"Sounds good. I'll see you there."

"Thanks for calling," Lizzie said before hanging up the phone.

"Thank you, Mr. Raymont, for keeping your landline," I said to the air.

"You are welcome, Faith," a voice responded. It wasn't the voice from earlier. I looked to my left. I looked to my right. No one was there. "Is that you, Mr. Raymont?"

No answer.

"Who said that?" I looked around again.

Silence.

So now, I was not only anxious about a serial killer dogging me, but I was also crazy. Great. None of this happened. I was just running on too little sleep.

I ran upstairs, where Sampson lay in a pile of pillow snow on my bed. He smiled from ear to ear—his tail wagging and brushing snow onto the floor with each sweep. I wanted to yell at him, but my baby was so darn cute with a piece of white stuffing still attached to his black nose. He'd torn apart two pillows already this morning and was working on the third. If we were going to be partners, Sampson needed to learn some manners. I googled Dog Obedience Classes.

# CHAPTER 20

I arrived first and was shown to a table in the back. I'd forgotten how much I enjoyed the restaurant's atmosphere with the wooden booths and the Tiffany lampshades. The building's depth and the darker ambiance worked to create a sense of walking away from your cares and treating yourself to fantastic food.

When it was warm, the open-air patio was an excellent option too. The front step was my only Feng Shui issue. Typically, you want as few barriers between you and your customers as possible, but in Doc's case, the step only added to the feeling of escape.

Years ago, I'd run away from the area so fast and far I'd forgotten what I'd run from. Yes, my family was crazy, and at the time, I needed a market for my skills, but in my mind, I'd run away from everything Michiana had to offer. I didn't realize what I'd left.

I'm rambling. I know, but I'm nervous. Yesterday's encounter had my stomach tied in knots.

I'd decided on a juicy cheeseburger, fries, and a salad when I saw the door open, and Lizzie floated through it. She'd always moved with an athletic grace I envied. While I communed with nature, Lizzie conquered it. It was no surprise she'd become a sports photographer, specializ-

ing in out of arena sports. Her photos of long-distance
runners, sailboats, and fishermen appeared on the most
prominent magazines' covers.

As she approached the table, tears streamed down my
cheeks. Hers too. My arms encircled her, and hers over
mine. It felt wonderful to hold my old friend and lend her
any healing energy I had. Not that my energy was the best
right now. But Chi could funnel what I had and give it to
her in a healing manner. Anyhow, that was my belief.

"I am so glad you called," Lizzie said. "I felt horrible
about all the things I said. Charles had me so wound up.
I am so sorry." She fiddled with her napkin as she said the
words.

"And I am so sorry about your father. Once I realized
who I would see, I couldn't wait to surprise your dad. He
meant so much to me as a child."

She reached across the table and took my hand.

"He always loved having you around. After the divorce,
my mother found numerous ways to keep me from him.
We grew apart. About two years ago, we decided to try
to start over. And it was good. Charles didn't care for
my father, and dad knew it, but I vowed I would not let
another person keep me from my father. But someone
did."

"What didn't Charles like about your dad, if I may ask?"

"My father is," she paused. "My father was larger than
life and loved everyone. Charles is a behind-the-scenes type
of person, and he doesn't like people. The two clashed.
Charles and my stepfather have a good relationship."

I couldn't help thinking Charles liked her stepdad's
money and position more than he liked her stepfather.

"How's your mom?" I asked.

"Mom's failing. Her mind. She and my stepfather had a rocky relationship. She'd never admit it, but she was happier with my dad. Private duty nurses care for her around the clock. It gets harder and harder for me to see her." Her voice trailed off for a second. "But enough about me. How have you survived? Charles learned a killer is stalking you."

"Do you know where he heard that?"

Lizzie's eyes shifted from side to side for a few seconds.

"I believe the owner of your company was Charles' client. He heard the news from the client's wife."

"So, Lenora told Charles about the Cash Crescent's death."

Lizzie nodded.

"I believe that's correct."

This was a lead worth following up. I never trusted Lenora. There was always something shifty about her.

"You still haven't told me how you are doing?" Lizzie said.

"Well, I'm taking some time off. I decided to come home and re-establish my relationship with my family. Just today, I admitted to myself I'm having trouble with anxiety. It's clouding my thinking, and I'm afraid it's stunting my gift."

I hadn't meant to share that. I hadn't realized I'd felt that way until the words were out of my mouth. But there they were, out in the open.

Lizzie's phone rang.

"It's Charles."

Her whole body tensed. Reading her body language, my intuition told me her relationship with Charles was not all wine and roses. She'd grown pale all of a sudden and held her stomach. I'd had a few of those relationships.

Thank Goodness my fear of commitment had scared me off before I made any rash decisions and married one of those jokers.

# CHAPTER 21

After Charles's call, Lizzie's whole demeanor changed. Her posture slumped. She avoided eye contact. Gone was the spark in her. The conversation came almost to a standstill. She'd gone on the defensive.

I was amazed when she allowed me to take her arm. We walked arm in arm out the backdoor to our cars in the municipal parking lot. The thought struck me that if I was going to stay; I needed to buy a car. I'd been taken care of by my company for so long; I needed to rebuild my independence.

As we rounded a row of cars, a loud noise sliced through the roar of the traffic. A windshield broke behind us. Another noise. This time, I knew what it was. I pulled Lizzie behind a car.

Special Agent Harvey Wallbanger came from the backdoor of Doc's.

He raced towards us. "Get down. Take cover."

One more shot. Harvey went down. Police officers from the station across the street appeared. They'd taken cover behind the Fallen Officers Monument. Two officers ran across Union Street, dodging traffic as they moved. Paramedics were only a couple blocks away unless they'd moved the fire station since I'd lived in the area. I reached for Harvey's hands and pulled him towards us. He had a pulse. That was good. And then we were surrounded by cops. My body stayed wrapped next to Lizzie's as my hands held Harvey's.

Another body. Lizzie had been right. I was death waiting to happen. Anyone near me was doomed. The best thing for me to do was leave. Disappear. Even Sampson wasn't safe with me around.

The question was, when should I leave? How should I leave? Where should I go? Arie would take care of Sampson. Should I leave a note? Or just go home and pack. And what about Lizzie? Now, not only had her father been killed, but someone had just taken a shot at us. Who had I hurt so much they wanted me dead? There were no jilted boyfriends or angry clients in my past. Not that I knew of anyhow. My clients loved my work based on feedback reports.

I never took a commission. I was the highest-paid consultant in the company. My nemesis at the company hated me. Did she hate me enough to murder people and set me up to take the fall? That was a bit extreme. Why shoot at me now? I'd already resigned. What would be her point?

Lenora, my murdered boss's wife, said if I'd been on time, her husband might not be dead. But she knew me. I got lost A LOT, and they'd started telling me the wrong time, so I'd be on time. So, I hadn't done anything out of the ordinary on his consult.

Lizzie. I needed to think about Lizzie. Would she be safe from Charles when she arrived home? There was no way he wouldn't learn she'd been with me.

I snapped back out of my stupor.

"Lizzie, will you be safe going back to Raymont Manor?"

She hadn't moved since we'd crouched behind the car.

"Physically. Charles doesn't hit me. He has other tactics," she said.

Somehow, Blake and Arie were now on the scene. A paramedic took Harvey's hands from mine before they moved him onto a gurney.

"What are his chances?" I asked.

"As long as there's a pulse, there's always hope," the paramedic said, stretching his neck.

Unfortunately, his body language told another story. The paramedic didn't think Harvey would make it.

A part of me felt grief for the man I'd known. Another part felt guilt. His death was my fault. A part of me felt relief. He wouldn't be dogging me anymore. Yet he'd taken a bullet to protect Lizzie and me.

# CHAPTER 22

A few hours later, I walked up the steps to my house. Someday, fate would let me live in my home in Abracadabra. But not now.

Arie and Blake were still tied up at the crime scene. Arie wanted a guard on me constantly, but we compromised on extra patrols in the neighborhood after a small battle. Now, all I needed to do was figure out the patrol's timetable, and I could disappear before anyone became aware. I couldn't live like this anymore.

Someone used my West Coast Trail of Death to cover up the murder at Raymont Manor. I was convinced. My money was on Charles. When I was away from here, I'd find out more about Charles Makey.

I needed to know if Charles and Lizzie flew in on the same flight. Once I was hidden away, I'd call Arie and give him the information I'd gained from Lizzie. When I'd left her an hour ago, she'd said almost nothing about the shooting—only answering the officer's questions with yes and no answers. An officer drove her home at Charles's insistence. Supposedly, he'd seen the story on the news while on a break from his meeting in Chicago.

While we were waiting at the crime scene, Lizzie received a text from her daughter Evie. Evie was fifteen. Since I was sitting next to Lizzie with her hand grasping my arm, I could see the texts. If I had talked to my mother, aunt, or Grams the way Evie talked to Lizzie, I'd have been tied to a fence post for all eternity.

With the death of Mr. Raymont, Lizzie lost the only family member in her corner. In contrast, I seemed to be gaining corners with my family. Somewhere in the cosmos, a reason must exist. I didn't have time to think about the universe. I needed to be on my way out of Abracadabra before my serial killer found their next target.

I finished a note to Arie two hours later and left it on the counter. When I was far enough away, I would text him and ask him to water Sampson and tell him there was a note on the counter. Tears ran from my eyes. I wanted to stay and be a part of my dysfunctional family. I told my brother about the flower farm I would someday come home to start and how I wanted to be there for my niece as she grew into a woman. But that would have to wait until the killer had been caught. Or had killed me. I didn't put the last sentence in the letter.

I couldn't let that killer get to my family. I just couldn't. I needed to get away, so they'd be safe.

After packing, I sat on the step outside and threw stick after stick for Sampson to fetch. He ran with his trophy in his mouth and made me chase him. I was going to miss this little guy. We'd only been together a short time, but already he owned a considerable part of my heart. How could I leave such a cutie?

How could I stay? He'd be a target, and I couldn't bear the thought of someone hurting him to get to me. As I played with Sampson, I noticed my protective patrol passed by every twenty minutes. I would wait until dark. Just in case Arie had someone in place, I couldn't see.

Sampson and I ate supper, and I petted him until my arm was sore.

As soon as darkness fell, I closed the door to the bedrooms and let myself out of the house. It was time to make my getaway.

# CHAPTER 23

After the next patrol passed, I grabbed my suitcase and walked out the front door.

With tears streaming down my face, I tried to open the trunk. A note was stuck between the lid and the bumper.

"Check Driver's side rear tire." It was written on the back of a card reading, "Vito Bracken."

I peeked around the car and threw my keys at a tree. My tire was gone. Another business card said. "Come see me. No me, no tire."

This was why I didn't do family.

# CHAPTER 24

"I'm going to kill him," I told Sampson on the walk to Dad's. I figured the pup could help me bury the body. Sampson was glad to explore new territory. I thought the half-mile walk to my father's house might cool me off. It wasn't working.

"Be careful, Faith. The wind has ears," said the voice. I looked around. Again, no one. I was getting tired of something I couldn't see commenting on my thoughts. It was like social media, except at least there, you had names and icons. Many were fake, but it was better than a disembodied voice. Plus, social media had a delete key.

"Who are you? What do you want?"

A brown rabbit scurried across my path. Sampson tried to chase. I pulled back and almost lost my balance on a thin piece of ice. Great, I could have broken my neck out here, and no one would know. It would be Dad's fault.

He dared to wave from his porch as I approached. Dad was 4'10", bald, and round, but his presence invaded your space ten feet away. He, like Mr. Raymont, was larger than life.

He held out his arms for a hug.

"Don't even think about it," I said, standing at the bottom of the steps.

"I see you got my notes." He sat in his chair—a pleased smirk on his face. He was enjoying this. He gestured towards the chairs.

"Sit, Faith, Sit."

In response, Sampson sat.

"Good boy, Sampson. Good boy," Vito said. "Your dog is well trained."

"Yeah, except he doesn't know his name."

"He will. Please, Faith, sit down." He pushed a chair toward me.

"Not until you tell me why you took my tire."

He sat back in his chair and took a sip of his soda pop. "I took your tire because I knew you'd try to rabbit. I wanted to see you first. You need to meet your niece, and your mother would like to see you."

"If I stay, none of you may live to see another day." There I'd said it. "I won't be responsible for another death. Special Agent Harvey Wallbanger died protecting me."

"He's not dead," said Vito.

I climbed the three steps and sank into the chair on the porch. "What? Are you sure?"

He gave me his 'father knows best' look. I recognized it from my childhood. "I'm sure. I have connections."

"Will he live?" tension knotted in my body again. Relief he was alive. Fear he'd keep on dogging me.

"He'll live. He'll most likely be riding a desk for a few weeks, but he'll be normal in a few months."

That was good news, right? It was. It was good news. His life had been saved. He'd been shot protecting Lizzie and me. I needed to remember that fact.

"I am glad he'll be okay. It doesn't change the fact that death happens all around me. Sooner or later, I'll bring death to Abracadabra. He'll hurt a member of my family."

Vito reached over and patted my hand. "You don't know that."

How much evidence did the man need?

"Of Course, I know that. I thought coming home would get whoever to show his ugly face by picking a new consultant to harass. Instead, he followed me home."

"Again, you don't know that."

Really?

"I don't know if the sun will come up tomorrow, but I plan on it. And I believe the killer is after me."

"Have you lived your life in such a way you'd be on someone's hit list?" he asked, leaning back in his chair.

See, this was another reason I didn't do family. Vito never revealed anything. He just got you to spill your frustrations, which let him see into your soul. Probably what made him a great mob boss?

"Not a normal person's list, but the fact he is killing people means he's not normal."

Vito reached into the cooler between us and handed me a root beer.

"Is this still your drug of choice?"

"Yes. It's 35 degrees out here. What's with the cooler?" And then realization dawned. "What else is in there?"

"Nothing you need to worry about. Your grandmother started you on that drug when you were just a baby. We had to watch you like a hawk because you couldn't read the labels and stole everyone's beers. One day, when you were still little, the door to a liquor store was open, and you tried to drag a six-pack out the door."

"Don't try to change the subject. I want my tire back."

"You'll get it after you've seen your niece and mother. You also have to say a proper goodbye to your brother."

"But." Couldn't he see I was trying to keep my family safe? Dad was a lot of things, but he understood the need to take care of his family.

"No buts. I will protect my family. Not your job, Faith. Your job is to help us raise your niece. And to help your brother see your mother and me through our senior years. And to raise this puppy who already loves you." He patted Sampson on the head.

Darn, I hated it when he was... whatever he just was. Maybe the word was fatherly. Not quite the word I usually used regarding Vito. Tears filled my eyes.

"I can't do those things if I'm dead."

"You will not die. I have connections."

I had no doubt he had connections, and they would extinguish the problem if Vito determined my serial killer's identity before the police or I did.

"I came pretty close to it today." As I said the words, a shiver ran up my spine. Lizzie and I both could have been killed.

He leaned forward in his chair.

"I don't believe the shooter was aiming at you."

"How can you be sure?" I twisted the cap on my root beer. I might as well drink it rather than hold the cold can in my hand.

"Because I know these things. I'm certain the shooter was aiming at Wallbanger. Special Agent Wallbanger thought so too."

"And you know that because of your connections, or did Arie tell you?"

"Both. It's not your job to protect the family, Faith. Go home and think about your choice. Your mother will be here tomorrow, as will Tiffany. If you want to leave after seeing them, I won't stop you."

"Do I have a choice?"

"No. But you can have another root beer. Did you notice I bought your favorite brand?"

# CHAPTER 25

Vito walked Sampson and me home last night. He said it was for our safety. Sure. He was just making sure I didn't call a cab. That thought occurred to me. However, growing up the daughter of a mob boss, I learned one of Vito's 'contacts' was never far away.

For a mob boss, Vito certainly had a lot of police-type information. Almost like he had a direct line into high-level law enforcement operations. Or maybe he was one himself. It was just a thought.

When I let Sampson out this morning, he came back inside with one of Vito's cards attached to him.

"Nothing Fancy 10:00. Be there."

Vito needed to modernize. People didn't leave cards anymore. They sent a text. And it would have been nice if he'd sent a car for me. If I followed the road, Nothing Fancy was a mile and a half walk. I could cut across the property, but it alternated between ice, snow, and mud in different sections.

Yes, it had been an adventure to walk from home to the Garden Center as a kid. Now, well, it was more like work. Expensive cars, dinners, and clothes had robbed me of my country girl fitness.

"Come on, Sampson. You get to meet some more of the family," I said. He trotted over to his leash, pulled it down, and sat on it. So, we needed to work on consistency. Well, two out of three wasn't bad.

Walking with Sampson was always an experience and brought me back to the wonder of my youth. Every twig, dead flower, or rock excited him and called for an investigation. While I knew my Feng Shui eyes were open, I didn't experience the thrill Sampson did at each and every item. Maybe I should. Perhaps that was part of the in-between.

We took the road for the first mile and then cut through the perennial beds for the last half mile. This bed would be filled with perennials of all types in a couple of months. For now, it was just tables and pea gravel.

A thin white-haired woman with bright red lipstick and earrings came from the back of the garden center. She was flanked on one side by a young blonde girl and Vito on the other side. I hadn't seen Mom in person in twenty years. But I followed her on social media. I'd kept tabs on her, Dad, and Arie from afar. No matter how strange they were, they were still my family. All that to say, Mom was looking frail.

Tears streamed down my face. What the heck was wrong with me? Trixie was the woman who dropped me off at my aunt's house and left in the middle of the night. Or picked me up and brought me back to Gram and Gramps. Sometimes, one of Vito's henchmen transported me. Mom sent presents when the only thing I wanted was to see her face. So why was I crying?

"Trixie," I said.

She stopped pulling the dead leaves off a sky pencil holly and, without turning around, said. "Faith, you came."

I walked around her to face her.

"Vito didn't give me much choice."

She pulled off her gardening gloves.

"This is a beautiful specimen. I was thinking of planting it in your father's front yard. What do you think?"

"I think you only want it in front if you want to send a prickly message."

"I thought that's what you would say." She dusted off her hands. "It's good to see you, Faith. It's been too long."

"It has been a long time, Trixie."

She extended her hand.

"Come. I want you to meet your niece. She's in the greenhouse." She gripped my hand so hard I thought she'd break a bone. I noticed her uneven gait. Her hand went to my arm for support. Trixie, like Vito, had always been larger than life. While people feared Vito, they idolized Trixie. I had been her biggest fan. Seeing her frail was new and gut-wrenching.

Each plant we passed, she took a second to feel. Obviously, Arie hadn't told me everything. Something was not right.

Inside, I found a beautiful teenager watering the pansy shoots.

"Hey, Grams."

"Hi, Princess," Trixie said.

An old pain shot through me. As a child, she'd called me Princess.

"Come say hi to your Aunt Faith."

Trixie felt for a bench and sat down.

"Princess, why don't you show Faith around? I'm going to sit here a bit and rest."

"Sure, Grams," said my niece. I walked toward Tiffany. I'm sure the expression on my face said everything.

"She's losing her sight," Tiffany explained when we were out of earshot. "Brain tumor."

I wobbled slightly as the meaning of the words crashed through me.

"Can they operate?"

We passed through the sliding glass doors into the next greenhouse.

"They don't tell me a lot. But I heard Arie and Vito talking. They can, but it's somewhat risky. Trixie wanted to see you again before she had surgery."

"Why didn't she just call?" I said, more to myself than to Tiffany.

"I heard her tell a friend on the phone; she didn't think you'd take her call."

Whoa. Talk about a gut punch.

# CHAPTER 26

Shortly after meeting Tiffany, I told her I needed to process the news. I kissed my mother goodbye for the day, not forever, and walked back to my house. The information my mother had been holding off surgery until I returned sucked the life out of me. I truly needed to process.

Thank God for Sampson. He kept me as grounded as I could be on our walk back home. Trixie had been an absentee mother, but she was still my mother. And she hadn't always been absent. When Trixie came to visit while I was in Montana and when she and Vito were home with us in Abracadabra, those had been good times. There weren't many times, but there were a few, and she and dad always showered us with extravagant presents.

I wanted to feel hurt that my mother didn't think I'd take her call, but there were times in the past when I hadn't. But I would have called and been here if I knew about the tumor.

Which was a cop-out. If I didn't love Trixie enough to take her calls for little things, I didn't love her enough for the big stuff. That 'dried bone' had just fractured. Tears poured from my eyes.

"It will be okay," the voice I'd come to recognize as The Lighter said. "You are here now. You must fix now before you come into your powers."

"Don't you mean I must fix the past and what powers?"

"We cannot 'fix the past.' We can only fix now. As for your powers, you'll see. Burr, it's cold."

I felt my right foot step on the hardwood inside my house. My left foot was still on pea gravel a mile away. For a nanosecond, I was stuck. Then my left foot joined my right foot inside the house. Sampson was right beside me. How the heck did that just happen? Talk about being in two places at once.

# CHAPTER 27

A few hours later, I sat on the back porch, wrapped in a heavy quilt, sipping a hot chocolate, and watching Sampson chase a squirrel around the outside of his pen. It was peaceful. Then, I saw Vito's bald head peek around the side of the house.

"You're not going to shoot me, are you?" he asked.

Actually, I was almost relieved to see him. I knew he was real. I was still a lot shaken from the two places at once thing on top of my mother's brain tumor.

"I haven't decided. I may shoot you. Why didn't you call me? Why didn't you tell me?"

He shrugged. "It never seemed to be the right time. And can you please come over here and unlock this gate?"

"I haven't decided if I want to."

"Well, I'd rather not shout the information I have for you." The set of his jaw said he had valuable intel I'd want.

"Okay." I rose to my feet. "How about if I walk over there, you give me a taste of the info, and then I'll decide if I let you in?"

He laughed. "You are your parents' daughter."

Vito pulled a piece of paper from a file and handed it to me when I reached the gate.

"What's this?"

"I'll tell you if you let me in."

I unhooked the gate.

"When you said you couldn't do this anymore. I realized what you meant was you couldn't take much more. So, you and I are going to partner up. Kind of like that old TV show *Feather and Father*."

Wow, I hadn't thought of that show in years. Vito was shorter than Harold Gould, the father part of the team. But Vito could undoubtedly have given them some tips on mischief.

"Her father was always getting into trouble, as I remember it." I opened the gate and let him through.

"See, we are perfect," he said, following me to the porch. Chairs had appeared on the back porch as well. They magically materialized out of thin air. Amazing.

"Okay. I can't leave now knowing Mom's health. I can't let her care fall on Tiffany, who, by the way, is an amazing young lady. So." I couldn't believe what I was about to say. "As much as I know I'm going to regret this, I'm in with your crazy scheme."

"You are?" Vito's eyes grew wide.

"Yeah, I can't deal with any more death. So, tell me what all these numbers mean on this paper?"

I sat on the chair and examined the paper.

"It appears your friend Lizzie has been withdrawing $10,000 a week from Mr. Raymont's checking and household accounts. It comes out of various accounts on different days of the week, but the total at the end of the week is always exactly $10,000."

"That's interesting. Where does the money go?"

Vito grabbed a chair and pulled it beside mine. He leaned over to point. I remembered that aftershave. Those were good times.

"The more interesting part," he said. "It goes into what appears to be Lizzie's pass-through business account. The money is then withdrawn in cash at various ATMs throughout the week."

"Okay, but she is on the road a lot for her business."

"I know. The withdrawals are always made when she's in the city. The ATMs are on the other side of town."

I shook my head. What? "That doesn't make any sense. Are you sure Lizzie is the one making the withdrawals?" I know my questions sounded far-fetched, but the information didn't line up.

Chi buzzed around Vito. He was enjoying playing the detective. "It gets more interesting. The person who makes the withdrawals is always wearing a hat, gloves, and sunglasses." He pulled a photo from his file folder and handed it to me. The woman was the right height and build for Lizzie. The little wisps of hair peeking from under her hat matched Lizzie's color, but I couldn't see enough of her face to be sure.

"So, we aren't sure that it's Lizzie?"

He leaned back in his chair.

"No, but she sure appears guilty of something."

"Or someone is setting her up. Trust me. I know the feeling." At that moment, I knew what I needed to do. It was like some weird force pushed me. "I need to drop in on Lizzie at Raymont Manor."

Vito stood and opened the backdoor.

"I will drive you. My presence might put the fear of God into Charles."

"Well, that's good, because I still don't have a tire. I'll go change."

He pulled his phone from his pocket.

"Right, I'll see that the tire issue is fixed while we're gone."

# CHAPTER 28

Thirty minutes later, Vito and I were on our way to Raymont Manor. I wasn't sure bringing Vito along was a great idea, but he had my tire, so what could I do?

"Have you thought about how you'll make a living?" Vito asked.

"I'm sure you already know the answer. Financially, I don't have to work."

"But...." See what I mean. Vito was good at not revealing anything but getting me to talk.

"Spiritually, creatively, mentally, and physically, I need to work."

"And..." again with the one line to get me to bare my soul.

"And so, I'm thinking of turning my property into a flower farm." I floated that out there to see what he would say. For a mob boss, Vito knew a lot about business. And he was up to date on trends. Something Arie wasn't. I was going to need muscle and growing know-how. Having Vito's blessing would help.

"A Flower Farm," Vito echoed. "Those have become very popular recently."

"Yes, they have. A successful one would bring business to Nothing Fancy and the other businesses in Abracadabra, as well as Moon Lake."

"There aren't many businesses left in Abracadabra. Your aunt is considering closing her furniture shop. She's not all that happy with Shayla running it anymore. There's Candy's Bakery and Cafe. The florist closed their doors last month."

"I thought I saw a flyer for a new pet store on Arie's refrigerator."

Vito turned left onto the highway. Apparently, he knew they'd moved the roads.

"Yes, they plan to open this summer."

His not adding additional information was suspect, but I was more interested in my flower farm. I could find out the details of the animal place later.

"Well, maybe I can do something about my aunt's store and include a florist operation into my Flower Farm."

Vito pulled the car off the road into a convenience mart.

"So, you've been considering this for some time."

"I won't lie. It's been in the back of my mind for a while. At some point, before the bodies started dropping, I started feeling this call to chase my dream. I haven't made any final decisions yet."

"And now." Wow, he was good at the prodding.

"I think I'll call Aunt Georgia tomorrow. But first, we need to talk to Lizzie. We can't do that parked in this lot."

"Right." He put the car in drive, and we were off.

Fifteen minutes later, we pulled into Raymont Manor. Two police cars sat in the driveway. One marked. One unmarked. As we neared the door, Lizzie appeared, with Blake holding her elbow. For a split second, a place deep within me was jealous. Then realization dawned. Blake was arresting Lizzie.

I hopped out of the car and ran towards them.

"What's going on?"

Blake smiled for a second and then frowned.

"Nothing you need to be concerned about."

How many times in the last couple of days had I heard that phrase or a similar sentence? It was getting annoying. Really annoying.

"Well, I'm already concerned. So..."

"He's arresting me," Lizzie cried as Blake helped her into the backseat of the marked police car. He closed the door and tapped on the roof. The police car drove away.

Blake put up his hands in a 'calm down' gesture. "Don't worry. I have my reasons. It will be okay."

I crossed my arms.

"That's all I can say," he added. He turned around and stood inches from me as if he was waiting for me to say more. So, I complied.

"Well, she couldn't have shot at us. Because she was with me."

"I get that, but you said you thought there were two killers." His fingers brushed my elbow as he led me toward his car.

"This is crazy. She wouldn't shoot him. Lizzie loved Mr. Raymont."

He leaned against his car.

"Love and greed don't mix well."

"So, you think this is about money?" Vito said.

Blake nodded.

"I think I need to stop talking and get to the station to question Lizzie."

I started to object when he flung his arm around me and walked me toward Dad's car.

"You and Vito are both supposed to be in Abracadabra, under protective custody. What are you doing here?"

"I wanted to check on Lizzie."

"We have these things called telephones to do that. You think Lizzie has something to do with her father's death?" It wasn't a question, and I wasn't used to having my gift turned around on me.

Blake opened my door.

"Go home. Stay safe. Trust me to investigate this properly. Please, I don't make the money you do, but I'm good, great even, at what I do. And don't hate me if you don't like the results."

I got in the car. Vito climbed behind the wheel. Blake watched us pull out of the driveway and followed us most of the way home.

# CHAPTER 29

Vito opened the door to Michiana Major Crimes Task Force Headquarters. The energy in the place was stifling. How could anyone work in here? Fear, anger, and frustration were the dominant energies floating around the room. It would take a week with the windows and doors open to rid all the negativity and fifty acres of plants to keep it cleaned. No wonder my brother was always depressed.

Arie met us right inside the door. It was like he knew we were coming. We'd gone home to make Blake happy, let Sampson out to play, and then when the coast was clear, Vito and I drove here.

"You can't be here," Arie said with his feet planted wide apart and his hands on his hips.

"First of all, you should have learned long ago, telling me I can't do something means I will. Second, I don't need to be in the interrogation room. I just want Lizzie to know she has friends." Surely, he could understand my need to help a friend wrongly questioned about murder.

"Part of the interrogation process is to make people uncomfortable, so they'll spill what they know."

Duh!!!

"I get that. Trust me. I've been in an interrogation room or two. And it would have been nice to have someone waiting for me when I came out."

"You could have called," he huffed, standing over me.

"Fine, you are right. I could have called. But we aren't talking about me. We are talking about Lizzie."

Vito stepped between us like we were small children.

"Son, just let us warm a couple of chairs. We won't get into any trouble."

"Fine, you can take those two chairs, but you are both out of here at the first sign of trouble. I'll throw you out personally for embarrassing me."

"Have we ever embarrassed you in the past?" I asked in jest.

"Only every other day during my youth."

"And see how well you turned out," Vito said, taking a chair. I had a feeling we were going to be here for a stretch.

An hour later, a man in a suit knocked on the door, asking for Lizzie. When Arie told him she was busy, the man handed Arie a paper. Before he would accept it, Arie opened the form. His shoulders drooped.

"Well, spit it out."

"Lizzie's husband. These are divorce papers asking for full custody of their daughter."

Wow, that was quick. Charles Makey was a first-class jerk. Talk about hitting her when she was down. Sadness and disgust warred inside me.

"I knew I didn't like that rat," Vito said, echoing my thoughts. Vito was right. Charles was a giant rat. How could he?

How many times had Mom and Vito been divorced and remarried? It got to the point I'd lost track, but they never tried to pit us against the other parent. Never.

"When did you meet Charles?" I asked.

"I may have been listening when he was at your house."

So, Vito was my backup. I wasn't surprised. He always lived in the shadows.

"See, this is why we are here," I said to Arie. "To help Lizzie when you are done questioning her."

"Somehow, I never saw you two in the role of guardian angels," Arie said before his phone rang. He walked into another room.

"No way, Lizzie is guilty," I said to Vito. "But being questioned doesn't look suitable for a custody hearing. Something smells rotten. Too convenient.

"I agree. The next time I divorce your mom, I want his lawyer. I've never gotten divorce papers served that fast, and I have connections."

"So, are you two married now?"

"I think so. I've lost track."

Was he kidding? Probably not. It was best not to go down that rabbit hole right now.

I leaned over and whispered in Dad's ear.

"It is time we figured out who is behind this murder and take them down. I know that's Blake and Arie's job, but a little push wouldn't hurt."

"Somehow, daughter, I don't think Arie would agree. But what they don't know won't hurt us."

# CHAPTER 30

Five hours later, we left the Task Force office. I tried to talk Lizzie into coming home with me, but she insisted she needed to get back to Raymont Manor to be with her daughter and call her attorney.

Vito and I offered to drive her. In the end, Arie drove all of us to The Manor. I spent most of the trip with my right arm around her and my left-hand drawing tissues from a box and placing them in her hand. At times, her body shook with tears of despair. I wanted to wrap my hands around Charles's neck and squeeze. Why didn't the serial killer take out Charles instead of Mr. Raymont?

There was a lot more to the story. Lizzie had said Charles didn't hurt her physically, but he had other ways of hurting her. Those ways had something to do with Evie. Lizzie seemed to fear for Evie. Although, she didn't come out and say so.

As we drove up the lane to Raymont Manor, I could feel Lizzie's body tighten. Her head moved from side to side, searching for I assumed Charles's car. When Arie's SUV stopped, Lizzie opened the car door and flew up the front doorsteps. Using her key, she opened the door and ran inside. We ran after her.

"Evie,"

"Evie, where are you?"

Vito, Arie, and I followed through the opened doorway.

"Evie, anybody."

A woman dressed in a red pantsuit came into the foyer.

"Jane, where is Evie?"

"As soon as the policeman took you away for questioning, Charles and Evie left. I heard him talking on the phone. They were headed back to New York City."

Lizzie slumped. Arie caught her before she hit the floor. At that moment, I knew the murder had not been about me. It had everything to do with the dynamics of Lizzie Raymont Makey's family. One thing bothered me. Were all those bodies on the West Coast cover for Mr. Raymont's? Or was this a copycat? Probably a copycat because they'd left out the picture and bones.

My name, nor my company's name, had not appeared. So, was this just a lucky copycat? Every part of my being said. No. The fact that Charles knew my boss's wife pointed all the evidence at Charles.

Arie carried Lizzie into a bedroom not far from the foyer, and Jane called Mr. Raymont's doctor for her. As Jane and I sat with Lizzie waiting for the doctor to arrive, that sense or feeling or whatever it was of being in two places at once invaded my reality. While my butt was in the chair holding Lizzie's hand, the rest of my body was in the study watching Vito shuffle papers on Mr. Raymont's desk. He methodically and silently opened and closed the file drawers before opening Mr. Raymont's computer. Was Vito behind the murder? Was he clearing away evidence? No, not with Arie standing guard at the front door. Vito wouldn't do that to Arie or me. At least, I didn't think he would.

Two hours later, a patrol car parked outside Raymont Manor. The doctor who'd arrived and given Lizzie a sedative left. But not before he guaranteed she'd be out for the night and most of the morning. Jane, who'd introduced herself as Mr. Raymont's assistant, said she'd stay with Lizzie for the night. Lizzie seemed more relaxed with her than she had with me, so we left.

# CHAPTER 31

Earlier, I'd run inside Raymont Manor so concerned for Lizzie; I hadn't noticed the energy inside. But as I left, the word that came to mind was relief. Immense relief. My body's energy field had been in overdrive, protecting itself.

Vito held the SUV's door. I stumbled a bit, climbing inside. Dad caught me.

"Faith, are you alright?" his voice softened with concern.

"Yes, the energy of a place usually affects me upon entry. I ran in so fast it got me on the way out."

"What did you feel?" Arie asked.

Arie asking about feelings. That's a new one.

"Immense relief."

"Yeah, me too. I was never so glad to get out of a place in my life. And I've seen some horrible things."

"Wow, I didn't think."

"That I was sensitive," Arie finished my sentence.

"I was going to be nicer, but yeah, that about sums up my thought."

"We will talk about my newfound sensitivity another time." His voice was softer, almost breaking with emotion. I trusted he intended to keep his word. But it wasn't a topic for today.

Vito seated himself in the back. The question is, did the manor feel that way before Lizzie and her family arrived or after? I didn't go inside the last time I was here. My intuition said Lizzie's family brought the darkness to Raymont Manor.

"What did you two find? I know you searched the place?"

"I don't know what you are talking about," Arie said, pulling onto the road.

"Yeah, right? Spit it out."

The two of them exchanged looks.

"Just tell me."

"Okay. There may have been something in Mr. Raymont's desk drawer. It appears Lizzie was in and out of rehab for five years. She's been clean for two. About the time she said she and her dad reconnected."

It was hard for me to believe that the bright, chipper, fun-loving Lizzie I knew could be an addict.

"She didn't tell me about that." Regret filled my senses. If she were in trouble, I would have been there for her. But how would she know that? I hadn't reached out. I had been so busy traveling from one town to another. And I understood. We can talk about our physical ailments, but our mental anguish stays hidden. I hadn't told my family about all the anxiety I'd been feeling lately. It was doing strange things to me. Like I couldn't calm down. Even meditation didn't seem to help. I seemed to be on all the time, even in my sleep. One morning I awoke, and my covers were halfway across the room. I must have flung them off during the night.

"Did you find anything else useful?"

Vito leaned forward in his seat.

"Maybe I rifled around. It seems Mr. Raymont had been keeping tabs on Charles. He had a private investigator. Problem is, I couldn't find the P.I.'s report."

"You think Charles got to it?"

"If he knew it existed. He may have spotted a tail or something."

"There was also an empty file on Evie. Somebody took the papers out of there."

"How can you be so sure?"

"Because they left the file on top of Raymont's desk. Like they were cleaning things out in a hurry. The whole room had that sort of feel to it."

My anxiety was starting to rear its ugly head. Its favorite way to do that was to shut my brain down. It's like I'd hear information, and a warning would go off in my head.

"Does not compute," it would say. I had learned to back away and come back at it from another angle.

"There's too much stuff in my brain. I need a whiteboard."

Arie turned onto the highway.

"I've got one at HQ."

"No, I had all the HQ energy I can stand for one day. I've got one in my office at home. And home is closer." Funny how quickly I'd begun to think of my house as home. I was once again Faith Bracken of Abracadabra.

"I didn't realize you set up an office."

"I needed something to do to get rid of my anxiety. Arranging things helps. Makes me feel more in control."

There I'd said it. I had trouble with anxiety.

"With all you've been through," said Arie, "I'm surprised you don't have PTSD—the non-combat type."

"I do." There I'd said that too. My challenges were on display.

# CHAPTER 32

We'd swung by the Task Force HQ and picked up Vito's car. He pulled in behind Arie and me.

Arie swung his car door shut and followed me toward the house.

"Sampson will be glad to see you. I had Tiffany come over and let him out. There's a key to your house at the Garden Center. Sampson has gotten used to you spoiling him."

Was that a backhanded compliment from my brother? Did he approve of my pet owner's skills?

It was odd to think of myself as a pet owner. I'd been on the road for years. I couldn't even keep fish because someone else would have needed to feed them.

"That's a good thing, right? It's been a while since I had a pet. Thought maybe I was losing my touch."

I opened the door to fake snow everywhere. Sampson had broken through the baby gate and attacked a couch.

"Hope it wasn't an expensive one," Arie said, laughing.

"No, I was going to donate it. Guess I don't have to worry about doing that now."

"I think Sampson handled that problem for you," Vito said, petting my mischievous puppy.

"Remind me to move Doggie School to the top of my to-do list."

I showed Sampson the couch and the pile of fluff and patted his little behind, which he liked. So much for reprimanding him. I tapped my finger on his nose. "No. No."

In response, he wiggled his little butt.

"Oh, Sampson, I hope you don't flunk obedience school." And then I remembered the pet store flyer. "How long before the pet store opens in Abracadabra?"

"May first" Arie said.

"Oh, I don't know if Sampson can wait that long."

Vito placed his hand on my shoulder.

"Sampson can. You can't."

He was right. I wouldn't have a house left if I waited that long. However, it wasn't Sampson's fault. He was doing what came naturally. I needed time to focus on him. Teach him the ropes of his new life.

"Who is with Mom? I hope Tiffany hasn't had her all this time."

"Your mother has a helper," Vito said. "Trixie enjoys working in the Garden Center. The smells, the customers, and the textures. She's fine."

Vito loved Trixie. He had forever, but the two of them didn't seem able to live with one another under the same roof. While his words said she was fine, his drooping shoulders and tilted head said he was filled with concern.

"Okay, well, do you two want some coffee?"

"I thought you would never ask." Vito walked over and grabbed a cup from the cupboard. How did he know where to look? I didn't need to know the answer.

I started coffee going and found a tin of cinnamon rolls I'd purchased yesterday before I met Lizzie for lunch. Putting them on a plate, I carried them into the office.

Once the coffee was made, I picked up a dry erase marker. It was time to get down to business and get this investigation behind us. I had a flower farm to plant. I'd grown up in a garden center. I knew how to grow things. But in the garden center, we grew plants that produced flowers. A flower farm produced the flowers—different steps in the distribution channel. Although we did have a tree farm, maybe it wasn't quite that different, but there was a lot for me to know. I needed this investigation done. Out of here. Gone. Although, there was a downside to that. I wouldn't have a reason to see Blake. And I was getting kind of used to seeing Blake. Hmm.

My marker touched the whiteboard, and I started writing.

"Okay, here's what we know so far."

I drew a line down the middle of the board.

"The West Coast Murders were always on my schedule several days in advance." I put that under the West Coast Murders, as I called them.

"And the killer always left my photo and a bag of little bones."

"You said Mr. Raymont's consult didn't get scheduled until the night before. There was no picture and no bones." Arie added. I wrote those two points on the board.

"The West Coast Murders were always paid for with the victim's corporate card. Mr. Raymont's consult was paid for with a throwaway card," I said as I wrote.

"How did you know that?" Vito asked.

"I have a trusted friend in I.T. at my old company."

Vito crossed the room to fill his coffee cup.

"Somehow, Charles knew about your connection to those murders. And somehow, he knew Blake had Lizzie at Task Force Headquarters."

"Someone took a shot at you, Harvey, or Lizzie, right outside a police station. That takes guts, arrogance, and skill. I'm not sure Charles has the background," Arie said. "He could have hired someone. I guess."

Harvey. I'd almost forgotten about him. A few days ago, he was always on my mind.

"How is Harvey, by the way?"

Arie grabbed another cinnamon roll.

"He's doing good. He should be out of the hospital in a day or two."

Hopefully, by the time Harvey was back in working condition, we'd have this case and all the other cases wrapped up in a neat little bow. Harvey could find some-one else to haunt.

"Someone was raiding the Raymont accounts and then taking that money out in New York at ATMs. Someone who was trying to disguise themselves to look like Lizzie," Vito said.

Arie raised his eyebrows. He either didn't have this info or didn't know we did.

"Lizzie reunited with her father, and her visits to rehab stopped," Vito added. "Apparently, Mr. Raymont knew about the rehab visits. He'd hired a P.I. to follow Charles," Vito said.

They were talking faster than I could write. I had to wonder if the rehab visits stopped because Lizzie now had someone in her corner. The lone wolf against the world might make great movies, but it was nice to know people loved you and had your back.

"Lizzie said that my boss, the third victim, was Charles's client. That his wife, Lenora, told him about the murders."

"Faith," Arie said, letting Sampson in, "when you were late arriving at your clients' houses, you said you texted them. But then you said you didn't have their personal information. So how did that work?"

"Well, I obviously had their addresses and names. If I was going to be late, I sent a text to Bonnie, our scheduler. Bonnie called the client."

I stepped back and looked at the board. "It feels like there is one more piece of the puzzle missing." It was floating around in a hazy wave state just outside my reach, but I couldn't grab it and turn it into form.

As I realized that, Blake pulled into the driveway.

"Should we hide the whiteboard?"

I wanted Blake to trust me. A piece of me wanted to pursue whatever was between us. Did he feel it? My gut said yes.

"No, Blake's cool. He's taken a personal interest in this case."

"Because a member of his team has a serial killer for a sister."

"Sure," said Arie, getting up to open the door.

# CHAPTER 33

"Welcome to the party," Arie said to Blake.

Wow, he was good-looking. Not movie-star good looking, more ruggedly good looking. Arie had almost black hair, dark brown eyes, and a quarterback's rhythmic grace. Blake had more of a cowboy aura about him. Not as striking as Arie, but tough and in control. My heart did a little yippee as he took a seat.

"Wow, a whiteboard with clues and everything."

"We are professionals here," I said to Blake.

"And it shows." He studied the whiteboard for a second.

"You have something to share," I said, reading him.

"I do. Guess what Lizzie's stepfather did when he was in the military?"

I would have never guessed her stepdad was in the military—not in a zillion years.

"Something to do with military finances?"

"That would be wrong. He was a decorated sniper."

"Mr. Ashcroft was a sniper? I did not see that one coming." I'd never met him, but I'd heard Lizzie talk about him. Somehow, I couldn't imagine Mrs. Raymont marrying a sniper. Don't get me wrong. She could snipe herself, but she used words, not guns.

"So, are we thinking Lizzie's stepfather killed her father and took a shot at Lizzie?"

"I don't know that we are thinking anything. It's just a piece of evidence. Where it leads, I don't know yet. What I do know is I would love a cup of coffee and one of those delicious-looking rolls."

"Of course, where are my manners? Arie, hand Blake a roll. Coffee is coming right up. Those rolls are store bought. You'll have to come back for some of my homemade ones."

He took one from the tin and looked me in the eye.

"I can't wait."

Okay, so my heart had temporarily taken over my mouth. Now and then, it did that. I just wished it hadn't happened in front of my father and brother, who were trying to cover their smirks. Why did I feel like I was ten again and had a crush on Caleb Burtsfield? *Blake is Aire's boss. Remember that.*

It wasn't the first time I had a romantic interest in one of Arie's friends. Arie had warned me off the guy. My untested intuition had warned me off of him. My hormones sent me straight toward him. It ended with me screaming no, and Arie breaking a window to pull his friend off me. That event ended their friendship and my romance. And while I didn't learn to listen to my brother, I did learn to listen to my intuition.

I poured Blake a cup of coffee and handed it to him. His hand touched mine. Tiny pulses of awareness flickered between us.

"Okay, Bossman." Arie broke the magic. "Does Mr. Ashcroft own a sniper rifle now?"

"I'm glad you asked, Bracken. And guess what? It fires the same ammunition the doctors took out of Harvey."

"But there's a problem," Vito said. "A trained sniper wouldn't miss."

Blake nodded.

"I agree." Arie got up and grabbed a bag of chips off the counter. "But they did get away after shooting across the street from a police station. Shows confidence."

Blake put his cup down.

"Or cockiness. The shooter believed he could blend in."

"Did you find his nest?" I asked.

"We determined the shot came from the alley between the antique shop and the bar. That alley is a blind spot. We believe the shooter shot from the top of an SUV, maybe through a sunroof. No cameras."

"But we aren't sure the shooter was shooting at us. We could have been in the wrong place at the wrong time," I said, not believing it.

"There is that."

"But synchronicity says otherwise," I said, more to myself than the men.

"What is synchronicity?" asked Blake.

"It's a fancy word for no coincidences," Arie answered.

I couldn't believe my brother knew that. Synchronicity was too woo-woo to enter his realm.

"Don't look at me like that, Faith. I told you we need to talk."

"I'm just throwing this out there for consideration," Vito said, changing the subject. "Got a hard time buying a trained sniper missed from that distance. What if Ashcroft trained Charles? They are tight, right?"

"Are they tight?" Blake asked me.

I thought back, replaying our conversation in my mind. "Lizzie said Charles didn't get along with Mr. Raymont, but he did have a good relationship with her stepdad."

"Okay, so we need to know the whereabouts of Charles and Ashcroft at the time of both shootings." Arie took the marker from me and drew another line down the whiteboard.

"So, where do we start?"

"Officially, we don't start anywhere," Blake said. "The feds are handling the case."

"And unofficially?"

"Vito's going to contact his contacts," Arie looked at Dad. "While we do a quick social media search."

Arie knew something about Dad; I didn't know. It was time they told me. 'No secrets' needed to be our new motto.

# CHAPTER 34

While Vito, Arie, and Blake were inside analyzing the whiteboard, I stepped outside to make a phone call. I was following a hunch.

"Hi, Jane," I said when she answered the phone at Raymont Manor.

"How is Lizzie doing?"

The sound of a door closing came in the silence between my question and Jane's response.

"She is still sound asleep," Jane whispered.

"I'm so glad. I was so worried about her." I should have rehearsed first. "Um, I would love to get a gift certificate for her and Evie to share at a local restaurant when Evie is back with her. Do you know a favorite they shared?"

Jane took a beat to answer. "Well, the few times the entire family came to Raymont Manor, they always ate at Doc's. Not sure she's going to be up to going back there."

The Lizzie I remembered would return. She idolized their onion rings.

"I'm just curious. Did Lizzie's stepfather ever come to town?"

"I never met either Lizzie's stepfather or her mother. Mr. Raymont hired me soon after the divorce. I know Mr.

Raymont strongly disliked Lizzie's stepfather, and he had few good words to say about his ex-wife."

"What did he think of Charles, if I may ask?"

"Several non-repeatable four-letter words usually followed Charles's name."

I chuckled to myself. He was a kind man, but he said what he thought. "That sounds like Mr. Raymont." I didn't mean to say it aloud.

Jane laughed.

"Sounds like you knew him well."

The times I spent there were crossing my mental screen. Good times.

"I spent a great deal of time there as a child. How did he feel about Evie?"

"He loved his only granddaughter, but said she was spoiled. When Mr. Ashcroft took her and Charles on a hunting trip to Africa, Mr. Raymont came unglued. I'd never seen him like that. He called his old friend, who was a local cop."

"Lizzie's Uncle Joe." His picture flashed in my head.

"Yes, but he is not her real uncle."

"Right. He and Mr. Raymont grew up together. If I remember?"

"I believe that is true."

Jane seemed as if she needed to talk. She'd been with Mr. Raymont for a long time. Jane could have been more than just an assistant. Even if it never got physical, still that many years, she had to be hurting too.

"Jane, how are you doing? It sounds like you've been with Mr. Raymont for a long time."

"I have been with him since about a month after his divorce. He was a good man. I will miss him." Sniffles followed for a second. "Lizzie promised to keep me employed until she decides what to do with Raymont Manor. Charles wanted her to fire me immediately."

That piece of information didn't surprise me one bit. Charles Makey was not a nice man.

"Jane, if you need anything. Let me know, okay? If you are frightened, you call me." I gave her my phone number.

"Thank You. You are a good friend to Lizzie." She hung up.

I needed a minute to process and breathe. A part of me felt the need to slip into the in-between and put a foot in Raymont Manor. Check on Lizzie for my peace of mind. But I didn't yet know how to do that at will.

I waited. Now would be a good time for the voice to appear.

The Lighter, whatever it was, didn't manifest. Apparently, being in two places at once on-demand was above my skill level.

I waited another minute and then walked inside.

"What was that all about?" Blake asked as I opened the door. I relayed the conversation details to Blake, Vito, and Arie.

"Hmm, if he took them on a hunting trip, Charles and Evie must have some degree of firearms training," Blake said.

Arie was now the one writing on the whiteboard.

"Too bad you didn't ask if Charles and Evie were home at the time of the sniper shooting."

"Yeah, I couldn't find a way to add that in gracefully. I didn't want her to feel like she was being interrogated."

Arie nodded. "I get that."

"Okay, so Lizzie can't be guilty because she couldn't take shots at herself. That leaves Evie, Charles, and Mr. Ashcroft?" The fact she couldn't be guilty made me feel better.

"Unless Lizzie was working in conjunction with someone else," Vito added, squashing my feel better moment.

"Alright, I'll give you that, but who? Did you get anything off the photos or bones?" I asked, realizing they hadn't said anything.

Arie shook his head. "The only fingerprints were yours on the photos and the outside of the plastic bags. Lack of fingerprints at least tells us we are dealing with someone who thought ahead."

"My money is on Charles. I don't like him, and he knew about my string of bodies."

Blake came to stand beside me. "We have to prove it."

# CHAPTER 35

"Hi Jane, it's Faith again."

"Hello, Faith."

"I forgot one of the reasons I called you. Do you have Lizzie's mother's number? I wanted to call and express my sympathies. We weren't close after she moved, but I spent a great deal of time with her as a child."

"I do." Jane gave me the phone number, and I wrote it down. "That's very nice of you. I doubt she cares Mr. Raymont is dead. But Mr. Raymont taught me it is always good to pour kindness into the world."

"I think he taught me that too," I said. As those words tumbled from my lips, a dozen little one-line moral of the story comments came to mind. Such as "being on time shows respect for the other person." Or, "if people respected others, we wouldn't need laws and courts." Many of my life principles were built from listening to Mr. Raymont when I visited his home. He did pour kindness into everyone. He called it dancing to the magic. Somewhere along the way, I started to understand.

At this point in my life, I needed to be willing to dance with the magic that is or was my family and my home.

"Is there anything else?" Jane asked, bringing me out of my realization.

"Sorry, no. I was lost in a memory for a second. You know what? Yes. I have one more question. Lizzie didn't bring Evie to lunch. I was wondering why."

Jane took a moment to answer.

"Evie was with Charles. She and he are very tight. Lizzie and Evie have what would be called a strained relationship. I believe Charles is the cause."

"That is so sad."

"Yes, it is."

We ended the call. This time I had remembered to put it on speaker.

"I'm glad Mr. Raymont was there for you when I couldn't be," Vito said, his voice breaking a little.

"He was, but it's in the past," tears threatened to take over my eyes. I had blocked what Mr. Raymont and Lizzie's family had meant to me behind an emotional wall. The wall was crumbling. My own family was chaotic. I sometimes thought the Raymont's divorce affected me as much as Lizzie. Okay, not as much, but close.

"So," said Arie. "Faith, you and Mom had your battles. Can you imagine being Evie's age, watching your dad take a shot at your mom, and keeping your mouth shut?"

"There were times that scenario could have happened," I said, primarily to myself.

"Okay," Vito put up his hand. "I admit your mother and I have not had a normal relationship, but I never considered killing her."

"Good to know," Arie teased.

A smile crossed Blake's face. I was sure to someone who grew up in a typical household our family dynamic was 'interesting.'

"Got to admit there were times we were worried," I added.

"Part of the reason I became a cop." Arie's tone was light and humorous, but I guessed it held a blade of truth. Blake looked at the three of us. How much had Arie told Blake about growing up a mobster's child?

"Let's change topics," Vito said. "Call Lizzie's mother and find out where her husband was the day someone shot at you and Lizzie."

"I will, but first, I need to phone a friend."

All three sets of male eyes squinted.

"Don't worry. This friend can help." I grabbed my phone and redialed Blister, putting him on speaker.

He answered on the first ring. "Hey, Super Sleuth, I was just about to call you."

"You were?"

"Yep, Bonnie has come up missing."

"You are kidding!" I couldn't believe what I was hearing. So, this was about my company, after all. Who would take Bonnie? Was she okay? How was Bonnie connected? Did I somehow get her killed? The thoughts raced through my head.

"Nope. Her husband says he called the police. So far, they haven't shown up here."

"What does he know so far?"

"Nothing, except she didn't come home last night. Junior checked. Her purse, keys, and phone are in her desk."

"Wow."

"Yep. First, someone drops bodies in your path. Then someone kills the big boss. And now Bonnie. I'm going to have to start locking my doors."

"Blister, you live in L.A. You always lock your doors. You even lock your office door when you're inside."

"Yeah, but that's to protect my Zen, not my stuff. I'll keep you posted. What can I do for you, Hot Lips?" Blake, Arie, and Vito looked at one another. I shrugged.

"Can you hack a couple of social media feeds?"

"Do I go to the bathroom?"

I had to laugh.

"I certainly hope you do."

"I like this guy," Vito said.

"Who was that?"

"My dad."

"You mean your gangster father is listening? Ask him if he needs a techie."

"We'll talk later," Vito said through the speaker.

"Sounds good. Now I have to deliver to prove myself. Pressure! Who's my target?"

"I need three feeds hacked. Mrs. Candace Ashcroft, Mr. Alvin Ashcroft, Charles Makey, and Evie Makey's. So, four feeds. I need to know where they were at the time of Mr. Raymont's death and our shooting.

"Mr. Alvin Ashcroft. Isn't he a bigshot hedge fund manager?

"The same."

"Okay, Alvin, his wife, son-in-law, granddaughter. You want me to do the daughter as well?"

"Sure, why not?"

"Not a problem. I'll be back in less than an hour. I need to look good for my new boss. Blister out."

"I do like that guy," Vito said, laughing.

Blake scratched his head. "Is he like that with every-one?"

"Pretty much. I'm probably the only person who never got offended."

# CHAPTER 36

Fifteen minutes later, my phone rang. That was fast, even for Blister.

"Is the bossman listening?" Blister asked.

"I am," Vito said.

"Okay, I'll text these to you in a few, but I wanted to explain first. Mr. Ashcroft and his wife have been in Paris for the last week. No way they could have hopped on a plane, killed Raymont, or shot at Faith and jumped back across the ocean. Tons of pictures. Not enough gap between photos. Lots of live streams. Ashcroft likes his own face.

"As for Charles. He hasn't posted to his account in weeks. I ran his phone records. Don't ask me how. Charles's phone pinged off a tower in Mishawaka, Indiana, ten minutes before Wallbanger went down. His phone was in New York when Raymont was shot.

"Lizzie and Evie Makey were in the area both days. Evie's phone also pinged in Mishawaka at the time of the shooting, but on a different tower. The rest of the afternoon, her phone was dead, which is odd for a teenager."

Hmm, where was Evie? The mall, maybe. Why didn't she come with her mother and have Lizzie drop her off?

"I did some digging into Lizzie. She purchased another phone. Her number ordered the consultation for Raymont Manor."

I dropped into my chair. He had to be kidding.

"Blister, can you find any connection between Charles, Lizzie, and Bonnie?" Vito asked. His hand was on my shoulder. I couldn't believe Lizzie had ordered the consultation. The warmth from Vito's presence helped.

"I'll get on it. Bossman, are you impressed?"

"You know it," Vito said.

"That's what I needed to hear. Blister is gone."

I mean, I knew there was a possibility my friend could be guilty, but that reality had never become a probability in my mind. Dealing with the cold hard fact, she was in the area when her father's murder occurred knocked the wind out of me. My legs and arms trembled.

"Lizzie didn't tell me she and Evie were in the area when Mr. Raymont was killed," I said, more to myself to justify my ignorance.

"Did you ask her?" Arie asked.

"No, I assumed they'd flown in."

"Well, we asked her," Blake scratched his head. "Now, we know she lied to our faces." He wrote 'Lizzie lied' on the board. "Did Lizzie know where you worked?"

"Probably. It's all over my social media. She's a friend on my personal account. We didn't comment often, but I'm sure she knew I was in L.A. and what I did."

"Whoa, back up. You said a friend on your personal account. Why'd you use that term?" Arie asked.

"Crescent also created a business page for me. They posted the content to it."

"So, did they use your full name?" Blake asked.

"No. Just Faith, but it had to be created through my personal account, and I allowed them to be its admins."

Blake wrote two accounts on the whiteboard.

The whiteboard was speaking to me. I knew I saw a pattern, but I didn't know what it was saying. Yes, the other murders provided some cover, but those happened out west. If Lizzie was going to kill her dad, why call me? Why implicate me? Why not Charles? Unless she thought I was the killer. Did she really think I'd kill Mr. Raymont? Wow, that question hit me like a semi.

"So, if she booked the consultation, do you suppose she asked for you?" Arie asked.

"I suppose it's possible. I'm surprised Bonnie didn't tell me. None of this makes any sense."

"Well, Faith, you are always late," Vito said. My family was good at reminding me of my faults. "She probably thought you wouldn't get lost on your way to Raymont Manor since you'd been there so many times when you were young. You'd make the perfect patsy."

"But why kill her father? From what we know, she turned her life around after they reconnected. How would she have known about the trail of bodies? Not like I announced that on social media. You two didn't pick up on it, and I know you both follow me."

"Well, I have to confess, I hide you often," Arie said, petting Samson, who had climbed onto his lap.

"Wow, given that you rarely post, I find it interesting you know how to hide people."

"Our tech girl taught me."

Of course she did. I could guess what he told her about me.

"I see. So everyone in your office knows you have issues with your sister."

He and Blake answered in unison. "Yeah."

Arie grabbed another cinnamon roll. "And the word is had. I had issues with my sister. Life changes you."

I gazed at him for a moment, trying to read his body language. What had changed my brother?

"Great. So that's why people were looking at us—your crazy sister and fugitive father."

"Not a fugitive," Vito said. "I've never been charged with anything."

"I've always wondered how that worked?" I wasn't lying. Everyone seemed to know Vito was a mobster, but he was never charged. His 'connections' were excellent.

"Someday, when the fuzz isn't around, I'll tell you how I did it. I'm semi-retired now."

Arie patted Vito on the shoulder. "Sure, you are Pop, sure you are."

# CHAPTER 37

While we waited for Blister, I made us a quick meal. When we finished, Blake took charge of the investigation.

"I think it would be prudent for you to tell us about this Uncle Joe character," Blake said.

I'd been trying to rummage around in the depths of my mind to connect the memories since I'd heard Jane mention him. Uncle Joe was a long time ago.

"Okay, here's what I remember. Uncle Joe isn't Lizzie's uncle. He worked for Chicago P.D. until he was shot and wounded. Then he became the police chief in La Porte. That's all I know."

"Is a last name walking around in your head anywhere?" Blake asked, standing next to me at the kitchen counter. His arm touched my shoulder.

"Maybe it started with an M."

"Mazoronni?" Vito asked.

"Yes, that's it. I always thought of him as Uncle Joe Macaroni."

"He's based out of Chesterton," Vito said. "I've used him before. I should have recognized his logo on that bill."

"You're losing your touch, Pop," Arie said.

Vito glanced sideways. "Keep it up, son."

"So," Blake said. "Is this a call on the phone kind of guy or a drop-in for a visit?"

"Definitely a drop-in for a visit. And maybe I should go alone. He's not the type to talk to cops."

Blake scratched his head.

"I thought he was one."

"Exactly."

"You aren't going alone," Arie said. "There's the possibility all of this is somehow connected to you." He grabbed his jacket. "I'll stay outside. Blake can stay with Faith."

Vito fished his keys from his pocket and started out the door after Arie.

"No funny business, you two."

No matter how old I got. Vito could still embarrass me.

"Those two don't know how much they love each other," Blake said as my brother and father exited.

"Yes, I think Arie would be a different person if Dad had been around more. Of course, if dad had been around, Arie could be a mob boss."

Blake laughed. "Your brother as a mob boss. Can't picture it."

"I know, right?" I rinsed the plates and stacked them in the dishwasher.

"About that."

"You think it's a cover, don't you?"

He shook his head. "I did not say that."

"I've known Dad my whole life, even though we were estranged. I am sixty-five percent certain it's a cover."

"For?" Blake asked.

"Still working on that part. But with Mom in her state of health and me staying put, I'll have more time to figure that out." I handed him the last cinnamon roll. "Let me fill your coffee cup."

"So, you are staying?" Blake asked, searching my eyes.

I shrugged. I liked his eyes—a lot.

"I guess. That's what my mouth said. And when my mouth blurts that kind of stuff without running it through my mind, it's usually the correct call. I guess I'm staying and starting a flower farm."

He put his arm across my back and walked me to the couch.

"You know farming is hard work. Even farming flowers."

"What? You think I'm a spoiled city girl who can't trade in her Pradas for dirt under her fingernails?"

"Not exactly. I think someone who made $10,000 per consultation and did several a day will miss that lifestyle."

Where was he going with this?

"I know it's easy to say this, but for me, it was never about the money or lifestyle. I enjoy helping people, and the magic that is Feng Shui truly helps people. When I first started, L.A. was the place I needed to be. The market has changed. I may need to come up with a different fee schedule, but I'm not going to stop helping people."

"So, how does the flower farm fit into the Feng Shui?"

"Well, first, it would add a little magic to Abracadabra. Arie's Nothing Fancy attitude needs some spiffing. Flowers make people happy, and happy people create good magic."

# CHAPTER 38

It was nice being with Blake. He was easy to talk to and non-judgemental. My phone rang. I put Blister on speaker.

"Hey, sexy girl, is the boss listening?"

"Sexy," Blake mouthed.

I shrugged.

"Nope, sorry. He and my brother are following another lead."

"Okay, but you'll tell your Dad I did good."

"Depends on what you tell me, Blister."

"I scoured everything. I couldn't find a direct connection between Bonnie and Charles."

"But...," said Blake.

"Who's he?"

"It doesn't matter, Blister."

"He hadn't better be your brother, the cop."

"He's not."

"Okay, you had me going there. There is no direct connection between Bonnie and Charles, but Bonnie's husband and Charles both have lost big on the same online gambling site. Charles is broke, and so are Bonnie and her husband."

My heart sank, but I had to know.

"Who runs the site?"

"Looks like a crime family out of Mexico."

"Thank God." I hadn't realized my muscles had tightened, but they had.

"Wait. You were thinking it was your father," Blister said. "Don't worry. I wouldn't have buried the lede like that if it was your father—one more piece of information. Wallbanger took down the patriarch of the crime family. Put him in prison."

"So, whoever took the shot in the parking lot might have targeted Harvey and not Lizzie or I."

"Possible, yes."

Blake twirled his finger in a wrap-it-up motion.

"Thanks, Magic Fingers. I'll keep you posted."

"So, it is possible. Charles shot at Harvey in payment for his gambling debts," I said to Blake.

"Probable. But who shot Mr. Raymont? Charles wasn't in town."

"So, what do we know? We know it appears Lizzie was stealing money from her father."

"Chances are to pay for Charles's gambling debts." Blake found a corner of the whiteboard. "Raymont probably found out and shut Lizzie off, so Charles shot Harvey in repayment of his debts. I'd bet it's only a partial payment. When you get in, you usually don't get out."

"That still leaves us with why kill Mr. Raymont? If he had cut off Lizzie's access to his money, he would have cut off her access to his estate. Right? And why would Lizzie send me to Raymont Manor to find his body?"

"We are still missing a piece. Hopefully, Uncle Joe can shed some light."

# CHAPTER 39

Arie pulled his SUV to a stop in front of Joe Mazoronni's office, which occupied the street frontage of an old three-storefront shopping strip on the outskirts of Chesterton, Indiana. This place looks as I pictured, Arie thought.

"I could have driven, you know. My car is a tad more comfortable," Vito said, opening his car door.

"I always drive."

Vito closed his door. All but the top of his head disappeared as he walked to the front of the SUV. Old streetlamps cast shadows across the parking lot's potholes.

"Still a control freak, I see."

"I learned from the best," Arie said, zipping his jacket to conceal his badge.

"You mean your grandfather?" Vito shot back.

Control freak was one of the curses hexed on the Bracken Family male DNA, Arie thought to himself.

"Something like that."

Vito stopped. "Son, you know I wish I could have been there."

Vito was many things, but he loved his family and would do anything to protect them. Arie knew that. One of

Vito's "contacts" had always loomed in the shadows. Spotting those contacts had made Arie the cop he was.

"Yeah, Pop, you've said that. I'm over it. You should get over it too. Let's go see what this Uncle Joe knows."

"He doesn't know anything." A man stepped from behind the building with a gun drawn. Whoa, should have expected that one. Arie's senses were dulled by the conversation with Vito.

"Put that thing down, Joe," Vito said, walking towards the gunman.

"What are you doing here, Vito?" He held the gun but lowered it towards the ground.

"Need Info."

"About?" Joe stood in the path, blocking his office door. Joe was twice as tall and broad as Vito.

"The investigation you ran for Raymont on his son-in-law."

Joe pulled out a cigarette and lit it. "Why, Vito?"

"Because someone connected to the case took a shot at my daughter," Vito said, his voice low and lethal. "I want that person. I want him real bad, Joe."

Joe pointed towards Arie.

"This guy looks like a cop."

"He's my son."

Joe leaned against the door frame. "That's Funny. Who'd have thought Vito Bracken's son a cop?"

"Strange how the Universe works," Arie said. Faith had only been home a couple of days, and already her words were coming out of his mouth. She had that effect on people. Her phrases started invading others' mouths. Ever since she could talk, she'd had that impact.

Vito looked at Arie

"Faith." He mumbled.

Vito nodded. "She's doing it again."

"Family is family," Joe said. "Faith, I remember her. She followed Raymont around chattering like a chipmunk." He paused. "The short answer is Charles was deep in debt to a Mexican cartel. He used his wife's access to her father's accounts to pay his debts. Raymont cut Charles off."

"Did Lizzie know?" Vito asked.

Joe shook his head.

"Raymont played the long game, gathering evidence so Charles couldn't take Evie away from Lizzie."

"Because she'd been in and out of rehabs." Vito finished Joe's sentence.

"Something like that."

Joe's shoulders slumped, and he leaned more into the door frame. His eyes softened as he talked about Lizzie. He was fond of her. Interesting.

"Who was the woman picking up the money at the ATMs, do you know?" Arie asked.

"Cartel woman."

"You don't happen to know where Charles was when Raymont was shot?"

"First thing I checked when I heard."

"And?" Vito prodded.

"He was in a board meeting. The head of security at his company and I spent a few lonely nights in a foxhole years ago. Video footage puts Charles there. I'm certain Raymont died because he shut off Charles's cash flow. Charles doesn't know that as long as Lizzie is married to Charles, she's on a tight allowance. And if anything happens to Lizzie, the money goes into a trust for Evie. A trust controlled by the bank."

"But if Charles doesn't know it, Lizzie is a possible target."

Arie walked away and pulled out his phone.

"Good to see you, Vito." Joe extended his hand. "Glad you've got your family back."

Vito shook Joe's hand.

"For a time. Trixie has a brain tumor."

"That sucks."

"Yeah, thanks for your help. We'll let you know what happens."

# CHAPTER 40

Blake and I spent the last thirty minutes lobbying theories back and forth before his phone beeped and he checked the incoming message.

"What did that text you just received from Arie say?"

"How do you know it was Arie?"

"You turned away from me. Your hand in your hair. Arie wasn't wrong. I'm really good at body language. So, what does it say?"

"He and Vito are headed to Lizzie's house. He has reason to believe she could be the next target."

My hand went to my throat.

"So, Charles was shooting at her, too."

"Arie said he'd fill us in when they return."

I had already jumped off the couch and grabbed my jacket.

"Then we've got to get to them."

Blake was now next to me with his right arm around my shoulder.

"Whoa. We don't have to do anything. We've got extra officers headed in their direction, and Arie and Vito are close. We are going to stay right here."

"You think I'm a possible target, too."

His arms closed around me, and he buried my head to his chest.

"The thought just crossed my mind."

"I know who Mr. Raymont's killer is. It's like that movie."

"What movie?" He asked, holding me. It felt good to be in his arms, but the magic was talking to me, and it would not be quieted. "The riders on the train."

"Okay, slow down. Let me catch up with that beautiful brain of yours."

I pulled away and went to the whiteboard.

"Okay, after Bonnie gave me the assignment to go to Mr. Raymont's, I called the office an hour later. Bonnie's assistant said she dashed out of there. She had to catch a plane to Chicago."

"So, you think Bonnie shot Mr. Raymont for Charles, and Charles took out Special Agent Wallbanger to repay Bonnie's husband's debt?"

"It's a long shot, but it's the only theory that works."

"Proving it is going to be difficult," Blake said.

I called Blister. "Hey, Fingers, can you do me one more thing?"

"Sure, this is fun. Is the boss there?"

"Nope, he's still on an assignment. But I'll give him a full report, and I am his only daughter, so...."

"Okay, what's up?"

"On my way to Mr. Raymont's, I was late and sent a text to Bonnie. Can you tell where Bonnie's phone was when I sent the text?"

"Can tequila get you drunk? I'll be back in a few."

"Thanks."

I turned to Blake. "I am not good at waiting. I need some chips. The crunch helps me focus. You want some?"

"I never turn down food from a beautiful woman." He followed me into the kitchen. I realized I could get real used to having Blake around.

Opening the refrigerator, I pulled a brick of cream cheese. "Can't have chips without cream cheese."

He started to open it. I grabbed the chips and set them in front of him. He reached around me to put the brick on the plate, and I looked up into his eyes. We stood there frozen for a second. I wanted him to kiss me. His eyes said he wanted to kiss me. His head lowered. His lips hovered less than an inch from mine. I tipped my head to meet him. Shivers of anticipation warmed my body. My lips touched his, and Sampson leaped between us, grabbing my blouse in his mouth. Seconds later, glass shattered. Blake pushed me down.

"Stay here and hold on to Sampson," he said, drawing his gun.

"Blake, you can't go out there."

"I'm going out the side door. Do not, and I repeat this, do not leave this spot."

# CHAPTER 41

For a few seconds, I obeyed. I opened the cupboard and shoved Sampson inside, using a bungee cord in the tool drawer to tie the door shut. Sampson whined, growled, and barked.

"We are under fire." I texted Arie.

"Do as Blake tells you." He sent back.

"So, like Arie."

I didn't respond.

"Use your gift," the voice said. "It's for more than Feng Shui."

We were in this mess because of me. I was not going to let Blake die saving me.

"Use the room," came from the voice.

Why couldn't it just tell me what to do? Why be so cryptic?

"You'll understand," said the voice. It had more faith in me than I did.

"Faith," Bonnie's husband said. "I've got your cop boyfriend. Open the door. Let us in."

"Don't do it," Blake yelled.

"I can't let them kill you, Blake."

"They'll kill both of us if you open that door."

"That's a chance I've got to take."

The voice had said, use the room, not the outside. When in doubt, go with the gut. I crawled to stay beneath the window and opened the door.

"Stand in the doorway so I can see you."

"Not happening," my mouth said. "You are going to have to kill me inside my home."

"You know I don't want to do this. I'm just in too deep. The cartel owns us."

"I'm sure they do. Why don't you let Blake go? We can all work on this together. Figure out a plan."

While they walked up the stairs, I poured a bottle of vinegar into the plastic cup on the counter and stuffed a Phillip's screwdriver from the drawer in the back of my waistband. Not the best weapons, but I had to go down fighting. Arie would never forgive me if I got his boss killed. I stood in front of the counter.

Blake came through the door first with Bonnie's husband behind him, a gun held to Blake's back.

"Stand next to her," Hubby said. Blake walked toward me and turned around. I moved closer to him, hoping he'd feel the screwdriver in my waistband.

"Now, say whatever you need to say to one another before I shoot you."

"Why?" I asked.

"You leaving the company presents problems. And your investigation was getting too close. Now, say your goodbyes."

"Can I kiss him one last time?"

Hubby's voice quivered. His body was jumpy. A professional hitman, he was not. He shrugged. "Sure. I'm a romantic."

I turned to face Blake. His right arm came around me. I moved the screwdriver from my waistband to his. My right hand found the vinegar. I leaned slightly back and hurled it towards Bonnie's husband.

Blake jumped forward, hitting Hubby with the screwdriver.

Sampson, who'd had enough of being in the cupboard, broke the bungee cord and ran full speed towards Hubby.

I screamed.

Sampson hit him.

Hubby slipped on the wet floor and fell.

Blake knocked the gun out of his hand. I grabbed it.

Blake hauled him to his feet and tied his hands with another bungee cord. Relief started in my shoulders and worked its way down my body.

"When this is all over. I'll take that kiss," Blake said.

"We'll see."

I texted Arie. "We are safe. Bonnie's Husband did it."

# CHAPTER 42

Moments later, chaos ensued. Siren after siren after more sirens sped down our little road and surrounded the house. Cars bearing the names of various law enforcement agencies lined the path almost to Nothing Fancy. Blake was caught up in the investigation.

I realized this was the first time I hadn't gone numb at the sound of sirens in weeks. For the first time since I'd met Blake, I also felt alone. Not because he wasn't here, but would I see him again? I'd shut Sampson in the laundry room for his protection. I didn't need him getting run over or licking every crime scene tech that entered my house. A thorough space cleaning was on my list for tomorrow.

Suddenly, I felt my right foot slide across the landscape and enter Vito's front porch. My left foot joined it. Trixie sat in a recliner by the window, petting Sampson.

"Faith, I asked the Lighter to bring you to me. I wanted to be there for you, but this tumor. You know. I can't do what I could."

"I'm here now." I knelt beside her. "You can have the surgery."

"That's a discussion for another day. Right now, you need to cry. You need to let all the icky stuff out. You've training to do. The Lighter and I have plans for you."

I wanted to ask her so many questions. But all I could do was cry.

# CHAPTER 43

Hours later, I came awake on Dad's couch to the smell of coffee and the sound of voices. Sampson licked my face. Vito, Trixie, and Arie were in the kitchen. My family was together again. Not all my family. Tiffany wasn't here. And a drip of sadness ran through my veins. Blake's voice wasn't one of those in the kitchen. I sat up.

"What's going on in there?"

"Hey, Sleepy Head," Arie said, walking from the other room. "Trixie wouldn't let us wake you. We stopped Charles's flight. He sang like a rockstar. He shot Wallbanger and was aiming for Lizzie. Bonnie killed Mr. Raymont. Charles believed he could break the will and sell Mr. Raymont's assets. Evie is with her mother and Jane."

"That's good news. And the West Coast Murders are solved."

Arie shook his head.

"I'm afraid not. Bonnie swears she had nothing to do with those. They hatched the plan to kill Raymont and Wallbanger as a copycat. But you no longer work for the firm. So we'll see what happens next."

Vito sat beside me.

"You are safe here in Abracadabra. We've got your back."

Trixie handed me a hand-sized black velvet box with a gold bow around it.

"I've missed some birthdays. Open it."

Inside, I found a GPS. "But..."

"I guarantee this one will work."

## THE END

## WHAT'S NEXT

What's next for The Bracken Family? Will Faith start The Flower Farm? Will Blake get that Kiss? Find out in Book 2 in The Flower Farm Magical Mystery Series.

## *SEEDS, SECRETS, & SUPERNATURAL* DESCRIPTION:

Faith follows the Magic.

...Blake is by the book.

Can Love Bloom?

They say when one door closes, another door opens. For Faith Bracken, in her second act of life, the door slammed shut and forced her back to the rural ghost town of Abracadabra. Now, she's staring at several open doors and trying to decide which one to choose, but the past she thought she left includes a body.

Speaking of bodies, there's a disembodied voice talking to her. Think Witch, Ghosts, and Alchemist rolled into one fifth-generation supernatural power. It calls itself a Lighter. It has a plan for Faith and her crazy family.

Blake's a cop. Captain of the Major Crimes Task Force. He's a good guy who is used to people doing what he asks, except Faith, her mother, and her niece. The more he tells them to stay put, the more they do their own thing— a thing that's likely to get them killed. Worse yet, they possess skills he's never seen, so locking them up for their own safety is not an option. What's a poor love-struck guy to do?

In a race against the clock who done it, Faith and her off-beat family need to solve a murder and save a loved one while adjusting to the new, more powerful magic. Can they solve a murder, save a beloved family member, and get justice before it's too late?

*Seeds, Secrets, & Supernatural* is book 2 in the enchanting Flower Farm Magical Mystery Series. If you love Paranormal Women's Fiction and Cozy Mysteries set in the country, download *Seeds, Secrets, & Supernatural.*

## LET'S STAY IN TOUCH

Keep up with all the news in Abracadabra, Moon Lake, and Echo Lake. Join *Kuhl News* and download *Blooms, Bodies, & Black Magic* free.

## A Note From Lucia

Dear Reader,

Thank You. I do so hope you enjoyed reading this book as much as I loved writing it.

For those of you who've read my Moon Lake Series, I'm sure you recognized Melba's Munchies from the Village of Moon Lake. The Flower Farm Magical Mystery Series will mingle with the characters from Moon Lake. I so love it when I return to Moon Lake.

In this series, I had the opportunity to write about everything I love. As a child, my grandmother's backyard was one big flower bed with a postage stamp of grass in the middle and a huge tree that grew horizontally. When my brother and I were small children, every so often, my father would take our pony saddles with us when we visited Grandma's and cinch them to the tree. We had real ponies at home, but the tree was also fun.

I'll never forget the look on Grandma's face when I 'weeded' her poppy patch and destroyed most of her poppies. She, unlike me, had magical poppy hands. Her poppies were always gorgeous. Mine just die.

Many years later, thanks to my wonderful friend, Jackie, I had the opportunity to work for a large garden center in Elkhart, Indiana. I learned so much about flowers, trees, bushes, and ornamental grasses. I will forever be thankful for that opportunity and the knowledge I gained.

I've always been fascinated by Feng Shui, magic, the paranormal, and the supernatural. Those 'this is going to sound crazy but' moments. I hope that love came through in this book.

To read more of my books, please visit my Amazon Author Page. I'm on Twitter, Facebook, Instagram, Book-Bub, and Good Reads. Those links are on my website LuciaKuhl.Com

Again, Thank You!

I wish you peace, prosperity, magic, and love.

Lucia

# Series by Lucia Kuhl

Current Cozy Mystery Series:
The Magic in Moon Lake Series
The Flower Farm Series
The Psychic Cat Series
The Ghosts of The Allegro Islands Series
The Mystwood Retreats Series @ Moon Lake
The Willow's Creek Murder Club Series
The Pair-A-Dice Psychic Sleuths Series

Coming Soon Cozy Mystery Series:
Glimmerton Paranormal Powers Series
Haunted Homestead Series
Destination Murder Adventure Series

19158460R00100